Matt c
Casey last enough

"Damn." He didn't need this reaction. Not now. *Especially* not now. She was the Colonel's daughter!

He remembered what she had looked like in her shorts and he felt another hot flash sear him. It didn't seem to matter to his libido that she was the Colonel's daughter. He still experienced the same hot, lightning-bolt lust that had blinded him when he was twenty-two. Then he could blame youth and arrogance. Now he should know better.

She was everything he didn't like in a woman: opinionated as hell, family oriented, and she despised the military. She didn't even like the man he owed more to and respected most in the world—her father!

"I'm insane," he muttered. But he was going back.

Rita Clay Estrada, cofounder and first president of Romance Writers of America, didn't start out to be a writer. She studied art and psychology, worked as a model, a secretary, a salesperson and a bookstore manager. But Rita's countless fans are glad she found her true calling creating enthralling, deeply emotional romances. As Temptation is celebrating its tenth anniversary this year, we wanted to highlight this very special author. She will be writing Temptation #500, available July 1994. Don't miss this very moving and unusual story from one of our best-loved authors.

Books by Rita Clay Estrada

THE COLONEL'S DAUGHTER

RITA CLAY ESTRADA

Harlequin Books

TORONTO • NEW YORK • LONDON
AMSTERDAM • PARIS • SYDNEY • HAMBURG
STOCKHOLM • ATHENS • TOKYO • MILAN
MADRID • WARSAW • BUDAPEST • AUCKLAND

This one is for a special man,
Ret. Colonel "Mat" Mathews. Thanks for your help,
views and especially friendship. This is a case of like
son, like father....

And for my Frankfurt American High School friends,
Tommy Van Doozer, Dave Rolin,
Whitey Fletcher, Curly Hunt and, of course,
Hank Richmond. And for Ann Conway who traveled
that newly paved road with me. All friends are rare, old
friends are gold....

ISBN 0-373-25574-8

THE COLONEL'S DAUGHTER

Copyright © 1994 by Rita Clay Estrada.

This edition published by arrangement with Harlequin Enterprises B. V.

® and TM are trademarks of the publisher. Trademarks indicated with ® are registered in the United States Patent and Trademark Office, the Canadian Trade Marks Office and in other countries.

Printed in U.S.A.

1

WHAT CASEY LUND NEEDED most was what the marines wanted—a few good men.

Even one would do. One with a strong back and hands, sinewy thighs and an artistic eye. A sense of humor and the ability to think on his feet were also a must.

It wasn't as if she was greedy. All she needed was one.

For her business, not for herself, she added. Between her boys and her stepfather, she had all the male companionship she needed.

Casey had started her landscaping and garden-design business over four years ago. It was something that she loved doing and it paid well. But now the demand for her services had grown so quickly, she needed help.

Mulling over the day's work, she pulled into her driveway and spotted Pops, her stepfather, sitting on the old-fashioned porch that ran along the front and side of her sprawling, two-story home. Casey loved this house on the outskirts of Houston, and the garden where she'd honed her craft. The older man held a book in his hands—undoubtedly one of his beloved Westerns—as he rocked back and forth on the hanging swing. From the swing's slow, steady rhythm she could tell he wasn't in the midst of a fight scene—otherwise he'd have been rocking as fast as the fists flew.

She surveyed the big yard, then the open, two-story garage. There was no trace of her two sons. She hoped they were out back finishing the lawn, which had been their task for the day. That kind of work was too much for Pops, and she wasn't about to pay some neighbor's child to do what Jeremy and Jason were supposed to take care of.

She walked around to the front and climbed the porch steps. "Hey, Pops. How was your day?"

The swing creaked and a frown wrinkled his weathered brow. Although her stepfather was in his late sixties, he'd remained youthful, and he couldn't have loved Casey more if he'd been her biological father.

In fact, the luckiest day of Casey's childhood had been when Ned James married her mother. Casey had only been twelve years old, but Pops, as she'd named him, had turned out to be the kindest, most wonderful man she'd ever known. Then, when her mother had died, Pops had moved in with her family, four years ago. He'd lived with them ever since, helping her with the business, and especially with the boys. Pops was "family."

"You had a visitor, honey," he said. "He wouldn't say what he wanted, but I'd bet it had something to do with your dad."

Casey stiffened but tried to pretend unconcern. "Why? What book have you been reading that would give you such a strange idea?"

"Wasn't any book, honey. Was a man in an air force uniform."

A cold sweat broke out on her forehead. "When was he here?"

"'Bout two hours ago." Pops rested the paperback against his chest. "He asked for you by your maiden name. Said he was a major in the air force."

Casey's knees went weak. She plopped herself down on the steps and stared at the darkening sky. "Did he say what he wanted?"

"You."

"Did he say what he wanted with me? I don't know a thing about my father anymore. I don't want to, either."

"He never said, honey."

Casey sighed. "Did it sound like he was delivering bad news?"

Pops knew what she was trying not to say. "I don't know. I was in the back room wrestling with that blasted computer program. The boys answered the door and got rid of him."

"What did the boys say?"

"Jeremy said he was glad 'the Major' left." Jeremy was her fourteen-year-old son. "But Jason wished 'the Major' would have waited until you got home." That was understandable. Despite Pops's presence in the family, Jason, her twelve-year-old, had admitted that he'd like her to marry again. He wanted a dad.

Casey searched Pops's face. "That's why they're not doing the yard, isn't it? They're being punished for bad behavior or for fighting."

Pops nodded. "They were yelling at each other so loudly that I thought they'd burst an eardrum or two, so I put one to work folding laundry in the sun-room and the other is cleaning the oven."

"That bad, huh?" she asked. Although her sons' behavior concerned her, she was more worried about the military man and whatever message he was trying to deliver.

She got up, suddenly too anxious to stay in one spot. "Well, I'll take a shower now and talk to the boys later." She leaned over and kissed the older man on the forehead, then went into the house.

Taking the steps two at a time, Casey hurried upstairs. The clock at her bedside read 6:55 as she stepped into her bathroom. She turned on the taps, tested the water, then flipped the shower handle. Quickly she stripped and stood under the spray, letting it sluice down her throat, breasts and abdomen.

Though her body moved with smooth efficiency, her thoughts were in chaos....

Her father. The Colonel. Her *biological* father—as a TV talk show would have stressed—was trying to get in touch with her. *Why?*

When Casey was eleven, her mother had divorced the chilling, autocratic man. Casey had seen him only once since then. On her sixteenth birthday, he'd appeared on their doorstep wearing a blue suit that could have passed for his air force dress uniform, holding a store-wrapped gift in his hand, and standing stiffly at attention.

With all the exuberance of a teenager who'd had five years to idealize her absent father, Casey had thrown herself into his arms. He'd patted her shoulder and then pulled back. That gesture had set the tone of the next two awkward hours.

Casey's mother, always a warm, fun-loving woman, had suddenly turned cold and distant. And when Pops had returned home from the garage where he worked as a mechanic, the Colonel virtually snubbed him, dismissing him as insignificant. He'd then begun issuing orders on what courses Casey should take, on what school—perhaps private—she should attend, and what college she should choose.

No matter how they'd tried to change the subject, her father had bulldozed ahead—until Pops had intervened, stating that he had to drive Casey to a teen church meeting. It had taken her less than a second to understand what he was doing, and to wholeheartedly agree to the deception. With a dutiful peck on her father's cheek and a wave goodbye, Casey had left with Pops, who drove to a local Chinese restaurant, then called her mother to tell her where they'd hidden themselves.

Within half an hour, her mother had joined them. Hiding the sadness of the circumstances, they'd laughed their way through the meal, trying to top each other with made-up Chinese prophecies.

No one had mentioned the Colonel's visit that night. Not even Casey. She didn't want to admit how it hurt to have her illusions smashed, her dreams of her future trampled on.

Much later, when Casey and her mother talked about it, her mother had insisted that her father loved her; he just wasn't good at showing emotion. Casey, still hurt and disillusioned, decided that mothers didn't know everything, after all. But she'd also realized just how lucky she was that Pops had become part of their family. Over the years, he became the father she'd always wanted. In handling all her adolescent emotions, he'd proved his patience and wisdom.

As she grew older, Casey realized that her father might have been right when, during that nightmarish birthday visit, he'd hinted that Pops had little ambition. Pops never worked more than he needed, never wanted his own business. Love and family were what drove him. But Casey accepted that. Like her mother, Casey needed the love and laughter of a close-knit family life almost as much as she needed air to breathe.

Jerry Lund, the man she later married, provided that atmosphere. Jerry and her parents fit together well. And it seemed to Casey, especially after the birth of Jeremy and Jason, that the three generations formed the perfect family.

Then her mother contracted uterine cancer. They were all jolted by the diagnosis; even more stunned by the short time it took for the disease to do its work. Three months later, she was gone. That was almost five years ago.

Shortly after her mother's death, Jerry was killed in a construction accident. Casey's beautiful family had been torn apart by death. She and Pops were on their own now. But they were still a family, with two wonderful—well, sometimes wonderful—boys to raise. Casey's business supported them, and Pops helped by doing most of the computer work and keeping the house running in a sometimes-smooth fashion. Their neighbors were close friends, becoming the aunts, uncles, sisters and brothers she'd never had. They had formed a different kind of family and continued on with life.

And if Casey sometimes felt alone and lonely, it was to be expected. After all, she was a thirty-seven-year-old woman who had been happily married and missed the closeness she knew was possible with a spouse. But she wasn't lonely enough to fall for anyone who couldn't handle her very active, extended family and even more active business....

Turning off the water, Casey stepped from the shower and wrapped herself in a towel, then grabbed a washcloth and wiped the mirror.

One look told her what she already knew: not a bad-looking body for an "old broad." The physical nature of her work kept her lean, and she often said she looked more like a runner than a woman who sat on the ground all day and played with mud. Blue eyes stared back at her. There were wrinkles at the corners, but that couldn't be helped; despite sun block, the rays took their toll, and squinting was one of the hazards of the job. But her breasts were still high, her chin was still single and her arms hadn't yet been reduced to flab.

"Mo-om!" Jeremy's voice echoed through the closed door. "There's a guy in an air force uniform here to see you."

He'd wasted no time in returning. Well, she'd lollygagged long enough. "Show him into the living room and tell him I'll be down in five minutes."

As soon as Casey heard her son's size-thirteen sneakered feet run down the steps, she hurried to her bedroom door and listened to Jeremy's explanation. His youthful booming voice echoed through the house. "She says she'll be down in five minutes, and that you're supposed to wait in the living room. But since she's just getting out of the shower, I bet she'll be more like half an hour, Major."

Vowing to teach her son a lesson in manners, Casey slipped into a pair of shorts and a T-shirt, donned sandals and then combed her wet hair. No makeup was necessary for this visit. And since there wasn't going to be another, she didn't need to worry about maintaining appearances.

Before the allotted five minutes was over, Casey was following her son's footsteps down the stairs just in time to hear Jason's excited questions. "Wow, you really flew jets? I've seen them at air shows, but I bet a ride in one of those things is outrageous!"

"It *is* 'outrageous.' But the years of training that precede flying take the edge off the excitement. Flying is a serious business," a deep male voice answered. Whoever he was, he sounded as if he wasn't used to explaining himself.

Casey smiled. The quicker the old fogy realized that whatever he wanted, she was too busy looking after her family to do anything about it, the sooner she'd be rid of him.

At the entrance to the living room, she realized that she had to readjust her mental image of what an old crony of her father's looked like. A tall gray-eyed man with sun-streaked hair stood in the center of the room. His at-ease pose was in direct contrast to the tight expression on his square-jawed face. If he'd been smiling, Casey was sure he could be the perfect model officer for recruiting advertisements. When he spotted her, a look of relief washed over his tense face. Dress hat in hand, he smiled with the confidence that she would welcome him.

Her reaction was the complete opposite. She stiffened immediately. His uniform was one that she'd recognize anywhere.

Jeremy started to ask another question, but when the Major raised his hand for silence, the teenager became quiet. Casey wanted to know how that "trick" worked, so she could use it occasionally.

"Miss Cassandra Porter?" the Major asked, his voice low and rumbling.

"Casey Lund," she corrected. "Boys, please go help your grandfather with dinner."

Their groans were quickly muffled by her fierce look. With sighs and under-their-breath mutterings, they left the room.

The Major began again. "I'm here on behalf of your father, Colonel Porter."

Casey crossed her arms. "I know who my 'biological' father is, Major. I want to know what your business with me is."

"Your father just had open-heart surgery at Brooks Air Force Base in San Antonio. He wants to see you."

Anger swelled in her breast, almost overwhelming her. "Really," she stated coldly. "And what makes him think that I would want to see him?"

The Major's dark gray eyes narrowed. "He was hoping that you might be compassionate enough to take a little time out of your busy life to visit with him."

"Why?"

His eyes turned to slits. She recognized the intimidating look from her father, but she was too angry to care. In another time, in other circumstances, his tactics might have worked. But not today and not for this cause. Her father had made her strong, not weak.

"You're tough, aren't you?" he said, his voice laced with disgust.

"I'm my father's daughter," she answered stiffly.

"I expected a little more compassion from a mother of two. Especially a widow. I thought you'd understand just how frightening it is to face death."

Casey placed her hands on her hips. "Did you know before you walked in here that I was a mother of two?" she demanded.

He looked her straight in the eye. "Yes. I know that your mother died, then your husband. Somehow I thought that might make you more understanding."

She was startled. She hadn't heard from her father since her mother's funeral, when he had sent a large arrangement of flowers. At the time, she'd been too concerned with the children, her husband and her stepfather to wonder how he had even known about her mother's death. She'd just assumed . . .

"I'm surprised," Casey finally admitted. "I'm so surprised that he'd want to see me that I'm speechless. But I still won't visit him."

"If that's your idea of speechless, I ought to introduce you back into the military. In our circles that's called verbiage." His tone was dry and rueful, and she couldn't help allowing a slight grin to tilt the corners of her mouth.

But her smile drooped when she heard Pops's hearty laughter and the boys join in. Although her anger had subsided, the hurt she'd experienced all that long time ago had not. "My father wasn't anywhere around when I needed his love and compassion, Major. He also wasn't around when I lost my own mother, nor when I lost my husband. He never even sent a condolence card. He wasn't around for any of my crises. Now you tell me I should drop everything and run to his side—just because he had surgery?"

The Major's answer was direct. "Yes."

Barely keeping her anger in check, she smiled sweetly, took his arm and led him out of the living room to stand at the front door. "Well, Major," she drawled, "you'll have to report back that you've botched this mission."

Opening the screen door, she dared him not to step out.

Still holding his hat in his hand, he stared back. He must have thought twice about what he was going to say, because he put the hat on his head, then strode out the door and across the porch to the steps. She saw his car, a tomato red Corvette sports car, parked at the curb.

He turned and smiled. It wasn't a gentle look. It wasn't even a friendly one. It was the look of a predator, sending a shaft of fear down her spine. "This isn't the end, you know."

So many things went through her mind, all blending into a feeling of deep and utter sadness for everything that had gone wrong between her and her father. Someday, she would have to come to terms with all those emotions. But not today.

"I know it better than you do," she said quietly.

He nodded, then walked down the steps to his car.

Casey turned to the long hallway that led to the kitchen. Although she heard the voices of her family, she couldn't help seeing the look in her father's eyes as he had said goodbye to her those many years ago—when he'd stared so hard, as if trying to imprint her face and that moment on his memory.

She knew that look because it was the same look she'd given her mother just before she'd died. All the love, memories, sadness and despair were there. And all the resignation that comes with the acceptance of the inevitable.

Blocking that thought from her mind, she walked down the hall toward the kitchen. If nothing else, the Major had brought home how much she loved and needed her family.

Although she tried not to think of it, she knew the Colonel's loneliness must be immense for him to have sent a stranger to ask her to visit him. But it was too late.

MATTHEW PATTERSON sat on the edge of the hotel bed and wondered why the hell he'd volunteered for this job. His old commander had been such a good friend and adviser when Matt had needed someone to lean on that asking Colonel Stanley Porter's daughter to visit him seemed the least he could do—and simple.

Matt was wrong.

If the spitfire he'd just confronted was any indication of the impossibility of the task he'd set for himself, he was in deep trouble.

And half that trouble had nothing to do with Colonel Porter—and everything to do with a tall, beautiful, in-command woman who wouldn't listen to reason if it fell on her head and gave her a concussion!

He had to believe the Colonel must have left out a little more of the story than he should have. Apparently, there was more than distance between his old commander and his daughter. Matt recognized bitterness when he saw it.

With more reluctance than he cared to admit, Matt picked up the hotel phone and dialed Colonel Porter's hospital room in San Antonio.

When the older man answered, Matt explained the situation. "And so, sir, I don't think you can count on your daughter visiting anytime in the near future."

The old man gave a shaky laugh. "She's as stubborn as her mother was."

Matt grinned. "That could be an understatement, sir. She's mighty independent."

"Was there any weakening at all, Matt? Did she look the least bit curious to know how I was doing?" It was as much of a plea as the Colonel could make.

"A little, sir," he lied. "Meanwhile, I'll see her again tomorrow and try to persuade her to visit."

"And the boys? What are they like?"

"Rambunctious as new colts," Matt stated honestly. "They help their mom some. Before I met your daughter, they were cleaning and folding clothes."

"They aren't a bunch of pansies, are they, Matt? Being raised by a woman alone is hard on boys. I wouldn't like them to be weak-kneed little guys."

"They're fine, sir. Your daughter is a strong woman who is a good role model, and her stepfather is an important part of the family, too," Matt reassured.

He'd forgotten how some of the older generation of men looked at things. He'd never been raised that way himself, but he knew others who had been told that any kind of housework was feminine, as if chores themselves had a gender instead of just needing to be done. "They were fascinated with my being a pilot."

"Good, good," the older man replied. Matt heard a breathlessness in his voice and knew he was tiring. "Call me tomorrow and let me know if I can look forward to seeing Cassandra, Matt."

Cassandra. Somehow, Casey fit her better. "I will, sir."

"I made a lot of mistakes in my life, Matt," Colonel Porter said with a sigh. "That young girl was the biggest mistake I made. I should never have given in to her mother's pleas that I leave her alone to be raised with another man as her father."

That was a type of problem Matt knew nothing about. No one had ever fought over him. He'd never known what being cared about was like. And he certainly didn't know what concern over "another man" as a father was like, either, so he decided that discretion was the better part of valor.

"Yes, sir."

"All right, Matt. Good luck tomorrow. Let me know what happens."

When Matt replaced the phone in the cradle, he took off his jacket and tie, then unbuttoned his shirt and stretched out on the king-size bed.

If he wasn't already so damn tired, he'd go down to the bar. Most women were fascinated by a uniform, and most men would strike up a conversation. Wearing his uniform was an invitation for company.

He closed his eyes. Instead, he'd get some sleep. He wasn't in the mood for talk—or anything more.

He was in the mood to dream of Casey Lund. To remember the fiery spark in her stormy sky blue eyes, the peach tint of her sun-kissed skin, the sheen of her mahogany-colored hair—and the heat of her hand as she held his arm, led him to the door and threw him out.

Damn. He'd settle the score tomorrow.

2

"A WOMAN WHO BUILDS koi ponds and waterfalls," Pops said with a wry shake of his head. "You couldn't have picked something to do that might be easier, could you? Something like chariot racing? Or first family of astronauts?"

Casey laughed and kissed Pops on his wrinkled cheek. "Not in this lifetime. Maybe next," she promised, reaching for the fluorescent-orange jacket she took with her everywhere, just in case. In case of what, she wasn't sure.

Neither mentioned the Major's visit. They had discussed it last night and then Casey had declared the end of it. Pops had shaken his head at her, but he hadn't pursued the matter any further.

Warm sun made her reach for her sunglasses the moment she slid into the truck seat. After a quick check of her tools, she started the engine and pulled out of the driveway.

She paid no attention to the sporty red car that drew up behind her and followed her down the street.

ONCE MATT FOLLOWED Casey into the prestigious subdivision, he lost sight of her truck. He got caught behind two vans and a private-school bus, unable to see her. He must have been crazy to believe that he could follow her and catch her away from the influence of her family.

Dressed in shorts, a T-shirt and jogging shoes, Casey had to be visiting friends, where he wouldn't approach her anyway. But he wasn't quite ready to give up. If he could drift around the neighborhood maybe he could spot her truck and wait for her to leave.

Matt wondered if she was visiting a man. He was surprised at his possessive reaction to that thought, and quickly squelched it.

Cursing himself for being all kinds of a fool and instigating this goose chase, Matt figured he might as well follow through. He cruised each wide street, occasionally marveling at the fabulous house designs.

Then he spotted her little black truck in a driveway at the end of a cul-de-sac. Casey stood at the back of the pickup bed, loading a weather-beaten wheelbarrow with gardening equipment.

Matt killed the engine and watched her as she wheeled the loaded barrow through the gate and disappeared into the large backyard. He waited for her next move, wondering what in heaven's name she was doing with all that stuff.

When fifteen minutes passed and she didn't return to the truck, Matt's curiosity won and he headed toward the fenced backyard. If she was busy helping a friend with a garden bed, it was too bad. He'd just have to ask to speak to her privately. He wanted to get this business over with.

He hoped his surprise visit would shock Casey into saying something—anything—he could repeat to the Colonel. So far, all he had seen was her anger. He had a feeling Casey didn't let too many people see the real her.

Whatever he'd expected when he rounded the wooden gate, it wasn't what he saw. What used to be a gracious formal lawn now looked as if a gopher about the size of King Kong had dug his way around the yard, burrowing here and there before forming a kind of kidney-shaped mud pit at one side of the yard.

He stopped and listened. The sound of a spade came from the back of the property and he walked around to it.

Casey. With her rich, dark hair piled on top of her head in a delightfully odd topknot, she was on her hands and knees in a shallow trench, carefully scooping out more dirt, then soothing the trench sides smooth. Her sweetly feminine fanny gyrated with each movement she made.

She'd surprised him again.

"Casey?"

She looked over her shoulder. "Yes?" She recognized him then, and her gaze turned from openly inquiring to stormy blue anger. "Did Pops tell you where I was?"

"No."

"Then how did you know where I was?"

"I followed you."

Standing, she dropped the trowel and brushed her hands on her bottom. "Why?"

He was surprised. No names, no accusations. Just a question. "I wanted to talk to you." He tried to intimidate her as if she were a raw recruit. "Alone. Where you can't pretend you don't understand or can't answer because of young ears or old feelings."

Her eyes widened. "I wouldn't use either of those excuses." She picked up the trowel and continued her work.

Matt felt his frustration rise. "You refuse to speak to me?"

"That's not the case at all," she said. "But since this is what I do to earn a living, you either become part of the solution or part of the problem."

Matt crossed his arms and glared down at her. Damn her, she wasn't even looking at him. "What the hell does that mean?" he finally asked.

"It means that if you want to take up my time with conversation, you'd better get down here and help out."

He had a feeling she meant what she said. "Where's another trowel?"

"In the wheelbarrow."

He glanced around until he found it in the bend of a trench. A shiny new trowel was mixed in with other well-used tools. Matt grabbed the handle, went back to where Casey was working and knelt down in the ditch.

"Now what?"

With a resigned sigh, Casey turned and explained the procedure, then watched him as he did what he was told. With a satisfied nod, she turned back to her own work.

Matt was surprised to find a certain amount of relaxation involved in smoothing the sides of the trench. He was startled when she spoke.

"So, what do you want to talk about?"

He pulled his thoughts back to the present problem. "Your father wants to see you."

"You said that before."

"Under the circumstances, I think it's only normal, don't you?"

She nodded. "It's nice that he finally realized he has a daughter, but I think I'll pass on this visit." She scooted ahead of him and began the troweling process again.

"He needs you."

"No, he doesn't." Her voice was tight with tension. "If he needed me, he'd have found me long before this."

"You're blaming him for leaving you when you were a kid. But you're grown now, Casey. You should understand just how hard it was for him to be with you when he had to travel to defend his country."

"Bull." She rocked back on her heels, fire spitting from her blue eyes. "He could have visited anytime he wanted. He chose not to then. I choose not to visit him now."

"That's childish."

"That's my decision."

"There's more to it than that."

"There sure is," she agreed. "I have a company to run, children to raise and a father, a *real* father who is not in good health, to look after." She stared hard at him. She inherited her father's ability to cut a man to shreds with a look. "In other words, Major, I already have a full life and am not willing to drop it just because the Colonel thinks I should follow orders."

Matt grinned. He couldn't help it. Spitfires weren't in his usual sphere of everyday living. It was kind of different and he enjoyed the change, even though he wouldn't want a steady diet of it.

"What would it take for you to spend three days in San Antonio and visit your dad?"

"The Colonel?" she corrected dryly. "Two weeks of hired muscle to help me catch up when I return. A housekeeper who would clean my house from top to bottom for the three days I'm gone. A cook to keep the boys and Pops happy during that time."

"You don't have a cook and housekeeper now."

"You asked me what it would take to tempt me into going to the Colonel's." She shrugged. "I just told you."

Matt rocked back on his heels. "If all that was done, you'd visit your father?"

Casey grinned. "Sure? Why not?"

Matt didn't waste time debating the issue. After all, he'd been sent to get a job done. If she agreed to visit her father under conditions he could live with, he'd completed his mission. Besides, it would give him time and help him decide what he was going to do with the rest of his life, too. "Done."

Casey blinked. "What do you mean?"

"I mean you'll have a maid and a cook for the time that you're gone. I'll hire a worker for the company for two weeks after you return from San Antonio. It'll take me a couple of weeks to make the arrangements."

She leaned back on her heels and stared over her shoulder at him. "Where are you going to find the kind of worker I need?" she asked. "I'm not talking about someone who just mindlessly gets a minimum job done. I need someone who can think on his feet. Someone who can follow orders and who has a strong back."

"Can you guarantee him room and board for two weeks?" Matt asked.

Her expression became guarded. "Is he trustworthy?"

"Very. I give my word."

Her reserve was apparent but he couldn't blame her. After all, if he was wrong, she was putting her family in jeopardy. Her emotions warred, but she finally gave in to common sense. "Okay, but you'd better be right about this guy."

"I am. I'll make the arrangements."

They continued working in silence for a while, traveling down the trench toward the wheelbarrow. An hour had passed before Casey looked up. "You don't have to do this, you know."

Matt looked at his dirt-stained designer warm-up suit. "I think it's too late. I might as well work until lunch."

"Whatever." Casey shrugged and turned her back, but not before he caught a shadow of a smile lighting her mouth. He grinned, too. She wanted his help but she was too proud to ask for it.

That was all right. He was enjoying himself. He'd been behind a desk or at the controls of a jet for too many years and the only physical labor he'd done was working out at a gym every other day. Helping Casey actually felt good, although he wouldn't admit it to her.

Several hours later, his growling stomach announced lunchtime and he glanced over to tell Casey he was quitting to eat. She was bent over the large pond area, measuring the layered steps to the deep end. In her concentration, she had stuck her tongue between her teeth and stretched long legs on the side of the hole, her face so serious he would have thought she was deciding the fate of the universe.

For one long moment, Matt was stunned by pure, unadulterated lust. Erotic desire caught and held somewhere in the pit of his stomach, stopping his breath with a hiss. A pure white light fogged his vision.

It was time to get the hell out of there. With quick, staccato movements, Matt stood and dropped the trowel, then headed for the gate as if the hounds of hell were on his heels.

"Wait!" Casey called out. "Where are you going?"

"To get something to eat," Matt replied over his shoulder. "I'll bring you back something!"

He couldn't get to his car soon enough. It seemed to take forever to climb into the driver's seat and start the engine, then carefully back out of the drive and head in the direction from which he came. It wasn't until he halted at the stop sign at the end of the cul-de-sac that he took in air and forced himself to breathe out slowly.

"Damn," he muttered as he turned the corner and aimed toward the commercial strip he'd noticed when following Casey. He didn't need this reaction. Not now. *Especially* not now. She was the Colonel's daughter, for God's sake!

Her image appeared in his mind and he felt another hot flash sear the pit of his stomach. It didn't seem to matter to his libido that she was the Colonel's daughter. He was experiencing the same lightning-bolt lust that used to blind him when he was twenty-two. In those days, he'd thought he was the hotshot pilot who could do no wrong in the eyes of the world. He'd had youth, stupidity and a sense of being invincible, then. Now, he knew better. He was older—wise enough to realize how much he *didn't* know.

Besides, she was everything he didn't like in a woman: opinionated as hell, family oriented and she despised the military. She didn't even like the man he owed the most and respected the most in the world— her father!

"I'm insane," he muttered, turning into a fast-food place and idling the car in line with several others. He was here to do a job, and he would accomplish it. She was returning to San Antonio to visit her father. Period. The end.

His forgotten sex drive and personal problems could be set aside for a few days while he helped out the Colonel. It wouldn't kill him. He was a big boy now, not that callow youth. He had wisdom and vision and common sense on his side. That ought to account for something.

When it was his turn at the order mike, he pretended he was Casey and ordered a light meal of a chicken sandwich without dressing and an iced tea. He figured that's probably what she ate because she was obviously conscious of her figure. Then he ordered his own lunch—a hamburger with juicy double patties of meat, a large order of fries and a thick, chocolate malted.

By the time he was back at the work site, he'd made up his mind he could keep his distance and still get the job done.

Casey stopped and peered into the bags he set on the patio table. "Oh, thank goodness! A man who realizes that not all women subsist on salads and bottled water," she declared, pulling out his hamburger, fries and chocolate malted. "I work too hard to eat lightly." She gave him an appreciative look. "If this is the way the military taught you to think, it didn't do badly by you. She bit into the juicy hamburger. "I'm impressed, Major."

Matt's mouth watered as he watched her take another bite of his hamburger. The woman in front of him wasn't the only thing he hungered for.

Trying to distract himself, he reached for the thin slab of chicken between a dry, whole-wheat bun and iced tea in the other bag. The smell of her lunch wafted around him and he gritted his teeth to keep from wrestling the damn thing out of her hands.

"Just part of my training," he muttered, and bit into the dry food. Somehow his taste buds didn't respond the same way they did to the thought of Casey's lunch—or Casey *for* lunch.

After she'd finished her food, Casey turned back to her work. By the time three o'clock rolled around, Matt was ready to call it quits. Besides, everything looked good to him. He glanced up to tell her so, only to hear the squeal of brakes from a large truck. After several racing engine noises, a man appeared at the backyard gate.

"You Casey Lund?" he yelled, scratching his tightly T-shirted stomach.

Casey didn't miss a beat. She gathered some of the hand tools and began placing them in the wheelbarrow. "Right. Bring the pallets back here."

"Can't get them through the fence—forklift won't make it, lady."

"At the gate will be fine," she answered.

The man disappeared and Matt heard cargo doors open and a forklift engine start up. "What's going on?" he finally asked, impatient with her for not explaining.

She looked startled, as if suddenly remembering he was even there. "He's delivering rock to line the creek beds and flagstone to form the waterfall and koi-pond area."

Maybe he hadn't heard correctly. "You line all this with rocks?"

She nodded. "Of course. Right after I lay down piping and thick plastic to keep the flowing water from seeping into the ground."

Casey left him to oversee the trucker. Matt watched, awed that such a feminine-looking woman could be so knowledgeable and do so much hard physical labor for a living. She amazed him. He had a feeling that the hard work was just beginning.

Unsatisfied with lunch, his stomach growled again. No wonder she ate his hamburger.

It was almost five by the time the trucker was finished and Casey was satisfied with the layout. Then the tools were washed and placed into the back of her pickup. She never explained that the day's work was over, but he knew from watching her that she was finished.

He decided to make sure. "That's it for the day?"

She nodded, her gaze glued to what was going to be the koi pond, whatever that was. Then, taking the wheelbarrow in hand, she headed toward the gate. "That's it. Thanks for your help."

"No problem," he replied, thinking she owed him more than thanks. She owed him a meal. He closed the gate behind them, then followed her to the truck and helped her load the wheelbarrow into the back cab, securing it with a bungee cord. "When can you come to San Antonio?"

He finally had her complete attention. She turned and leaned against the wheel well. "What?"

"San Antonio," he repeated slowly. "You said you would visit your dad."

She went cold again, practically chilling him with her frozen look. "My biological father," she corrected. "And I didn't say I would go. I said I had some problems to solve first."

"I already solved them."

"I haven't quite accepted that, yet."

"Yes, you did."

"No, I didn't," she retorted sternly. "I said I didn't trust the man who was supposed to help me."

Unused to explaining himself, Matt carefully held on to his patience. "And I told you he was trustworthy."

"How do you know?"

"Because I'm him." At her stunned expression, he felt satisfaction flow through him.

For once, she was speechless. "You?" she finally said.

He smiled.

"But, why?"

"Because your father was not only my commanding officer, he was my mentor. It's the least I can do in return for all he's done for me."

Lightning couldn't have spit more light from her eyes than her reaction to his words did. Her smile was as dangerous as it had been when she'd escorted him from her home. "Isn't it wonderful he was there for someone. It certainly wasn't me. Or my mother."

"You can only speak for your own self, Casey. No one else knows what goes on inside a marriage."

"That may be, but I know how he behaved around both of us. You don't."

Matt conceded that point. After all, he'd done the same thing with his own family. Judging and acknowledging what was good for you was subjective at best.

"I agree, Casey. God only knows, I don't have any answers for you. But I do know that he misses not having a relationship with you and wants another chance. I know that he cares about you and the boys, and wishes he could get to know them, too."

Her mouth opened to form words, but none came out. Matt knew he was on the right path. "He's still in the hospital recuperating, and may not make it through another heart attack. Are you willing to lose a chance most people never get? Are you willing to pretend your father will go on forever so you can continue to hate whatever he did—or didn't do—to you and your mother? Is that what your mother taught you?"

Her voice was low and choked when she finally answered. "You don't play fair, Major. The military rarely does."

"Keep the military out of this. This is between you and me, Casey. Either I persuade you to try something that might make you feel better after he's gone, or I fail. If I fail, I don't pay the penalty. You do." He hesitated a moment. "We rarely get second chances, Casey. This is one of those rare times."

"You low-down, son of a . . ." she began, so angry her hands were clenched into fists at her sides.

"I'm not the problem," he reminded her gently. "I'm the solution."

Matt could tell she had a few other things to say, but she must have thought better of it. Instead, she reached into her back pocket and pulled out two keys attached to a large medallion of Saint Jude. She stared at the imprint for a moment, then looked up at him. "Fitting, don't you think? My favorite saint is the one in charge of lost causes."

"He's a lot of people's favorite."

Casey turned and opened the truck door. "Call me sometime tomorrow night and I'll give you my decision." She climbed into the front seat and slammed the door behind her, rolled down the window and crooked an elbow out. "Until then, stay away from me, Major."

"Don't you want my help tomorrow?"

"I want help from anyone *except* you, Major. You're dismissed from duty."

She gunned the engine, slammed it into reverse and backed out of the driveway.

Matt stood at the edge of the driveway and gave a smart salute. But the grin on his face ruined the whole effect.

The Colonel would be proud.

Mission accomplished.

3

THE TRUCK HIT A BUMP and jolted Casey's attention back to the road leading to Brooks Medical Center in San Antonio. She wondered just how she'd been talked into visiting the Colonel.

She was sure the core of her problem was Major Matthew Patterson. She was certain that she wouldn't be doing this if she hadn't been the least bit curious about the man she'd once idolized and now regarded with disdain. *And hurt*, her inner child added loudly.

Fate, it seemed, had come to remind her that the relationship between herself and the Colonel had not been settled. But she didn't know what she could do to make peace with her father's ghost. After all, he hadn't been around for her to confront.

But instead of being able to tell herself that she was okay now, that she could forgive her father for having failed her, she still saw him with sixteen-year-old eyes, as he'd dictated to her mother what type of education she should have. It wasn't a pretty picture.

Casey passed the car in front of her and scooted into a parking spot. Once she'd turned off the engine, she sat quietly and stared at the multistoried building in front of her. Her heart was beating so quickly she took a deep breath to calm it.

It had been over twenty years since she'd seen this man. Twenty-one years was a long time. Would she recognize him? Would they have *anything* to say to each other? Could he still hurt her?

Tamping down the panic, Casey reached for her purse, stepped out of the truck and headed toward the entrance. She was here and had to deal with what lay ahead.

Uniforms were everywhere. Blue and brown, dress and fatigues, reminding her of the regimented lifestyle she'd come to hate as a child. Squaring her shoulders, she walked to the desk and asked directions to her father's room.

Once outside the door, Casey's feet refused to carry her any farther. She stood there, her hands frozen at her sides. Hospital employees bustled along the wide hallways, none of them paying attention to her dilemma. She wanted to turn and run, but couldn't even manage that. Her muscles were so tight she couldn't move them.

"It's not that bad, you know." Matt's voice came from behind her even though, for a moment, she thought she'd imagined it.

But her body knew better, responding instantly to the closeness of him by turning in his direction. "How would you know?" she finally managed.

"Because you're visiting a man who wants to see you. The Colonel is waiting for you, and probably just as nervous as you are."

For just a second, that thought loosened her tensed muscles. Then she thought again. "I doubt it. The Colonel doesn't get nervous. He gets even."

"That's not true."

"He used to say that himself," she protested, and Matt took her hands in his. Her hands were cold and stiff. His clasp felt warm and solid. "I heard him."

"That was only used to intimidate his men. Your father is just as human as the rest of us, Casey. And twice as nervous. After all, he was the one who requested this meeting."

Her eyes locked with his, silently pleading for more assurance to give her the courage to walk through the portal.

With a sigh, Matt guided her down the hall to a small bench beside the elevators. "Sit down," he ordered, taking her hands in his once more. "Your hands are like ice." Gently, he rubbed them between his own, giving his warmth to her.

She watched their hands, both tanned by the sun, both strong, but Matt's were larger, stronger, caring in their movements. She wanted to cry, but she wasn't sure if it was because of his tenderness or her deepseated and childish fear of the encounter still ahead. Perhaps both.

"I'm not chicken," she said, trying to keep her teeth from chattering.

"I know." His voice was warm and soothing.

"I'm just not sure this is the right thing for either of us. If he's as nervous as you say, what happens if he has a heart attack?"

Matt continued rubbing her hands. "Then he's in the right place, don't you think? No safer place for him than a hospital."

"What if he's changed his mind and doesn't really want to see me?"

"He hasn't," Matt reassured her. "I spoke to him just fifteen minutes before you arrived. He wants to see you more than ever." He gave her hands a squeeze. "Ready?"

She took inventory. Surprisingly, Casey was ready. At least she thought she was ready. Her hands felt as if they had circulation again, and her nerves were no longer numb and frozen. She wasn't shaking.

"Ready."

One minute later she was where she had started— in front of her father's hospital-room door. This time she raised her hand and pushed against the cool wood, stepping forward as it gave way to expose a plain, gray-painted room whose only contrast was the bed dressed in white and the man lying in the center of it.

He was staring straight at her, his blue eyes, so like her own, absorbing her from head to toe before seeking her gaze again. "Cassandra." It was a low, rasping sound. She would recognize it anywhere.

"Hi," she said softly, working around the lump in her throat. He looked so small, so pale, so tired compared to the vigorous giant of a man she remembered as a child. Hair once so dark brown it looked black was now scarce and mostly gray. She walked to the side of the bed and accepted the hand stretched out to touch her. "How are you?" It was a stupid question, but she couldn't think of anything else to say.

The older man's smile was slow in coming. Tears filmed his eyes and he tried to blink them away. "I'll be fine as soon as I get out of this damn place."

"It sounds like the natives are restless," she joked weakly, trying to pour all her strength into him through their hands.

"Aren't you going to give me a hug?" her father asked.

Her heart went out to him. Never, ever, had she seen him as a man who needed anyone. Especially her. She smiled. "Of course I am," she said, bending over to squeeze his shoulders.

Matt put a chair behind her and let her know by touching her shoulder. It was more reassuring than she cared to think about to know that he was with her.

Still holding her father's hand, she sat back, staring at the man she'd been so stubborn about meeting. "Is everything all right?"

"As good as it's going to get," her father tried to joke. "They inserted a pacemaker."

Her heart hurt at the thought of her father, distant and hard as he used to be, without his usual vigor.

He gave a weak smile. "I'm told I can't complain since I'm still here. But I have to watch my weight and do my exercises."

She couldn't resist a barb. "Maybe you should blame the military cooks."

"Maybe."

Matt touched her shoulder. "I'll be out in the hall getting a cup of coffee if anyone needs me."

Casey looked over her shoulder, silently pleading with him not to leave her, but he ignored it. Turning his back on both of them, he closed the door quietly behind him.

The Colonel sighed. "That's quite a guy, Cassandra. I have a lot to thank him for, including you being here."

"He seems very nice," she demurred, unwilling to give him the credit for her own actions. She could have said no.

"He's like the son I never had."

"I'm sure." She didn't know why she was surprised at the hurt his words evoked. She should have prepared for that subtle form of prejudice by now. He'd had a daughter and ignored her completely. Sons were the only family who seemed to matter to men like her father.

He didn't hear the bitterness in her voice or she was sure he would have commented on it. Instead, he changed the subject. "How are the boys? Did you bring them with you?"

"They're home. They have school and swim-team practice and races, and a social life that doesn't stop," she explained matter-of-factly, still unsure how to proceed. This was all new to her. Her only consolation was that it was probably all new to him, too.

"How old are they now?"

Casey stared at their entwined hands. His were thin-skinned, the veins visible just below the surface. Hers were soft—from the half bottle of lotion she'd put on before driving here—with short-trimmed nails. "Twelve and fourteen."

"That's a rough age for a woman raising boys all alone."

"I'm not alone." She couldn't resist that. It was with great satisfaction that she answered truthfully, "Pops lives with me."

"How could I forget Pops." The Colonel surprised her with his anger. "That old goat kept me from my family all these years."

Casey stiffened. "That 'old goat' happens to be my best friend, business partner and helper. And he *never* kept you from me. You did that all on your own."

"He never should have been with your mother. She was too good for him." Her father's voice was harsh and accusing. "He coaxed her away from me when I wasn't looking, that damned cheater."

Casey withdrew her hand from his and clasped it tightly in her lap. "That's not true."

The Colonel's eyes widened. "Do you think I'd *lie* about something like that?" he asked, incredulous that she would correct him.

Years ago, his look would have intimidated her and she would have remained silent. But not now. "Obviously, I do."

"Let me tell you, little lady. Your mother and that man were seeing each other while she was still married to me. I blame him."

"Really?" Casey stood, anger stiffening every muscle. "Why don't you try putting the blame where it belongs? On you."

The silence filling the room was accented only by her father's raspy breathing.

"This is silly," he finally admitted. "You had nothing to do with those days . . . or our marriage. I never should have brought it up."

"No, you shouldn't have," she agreed. "As I remember, I had nothing to do with you, either." Casey turned toward the door. "I'm leaving now." Her footsteps clicked briskly as she walked toward the exit, anxious to catch a breath of fresh air.

"Casey." Her father stopped her just as she reached the door. "Come back. Talk to me."

She couldn't turn around. Instead, with her hand tightly clasping the long door handle, she stared at the painted wood in front of her. "Not now. Maybe later."

"It doesn't matter what happened all those years ago," her father said tiredly. "Everyone knows what happened. Our marriage isn't classified anymore."

"'Classified'?" Casey's voice rose as she turned to face him, clutching the long handle of the door as if it were a lifeline. "It was never *classified!* Your marriage and our family were never a military concern!"

"You don't understand, Cassandra. The military was my life. It gave us food and shelter and clothes on our backs. Your mother never appreciated that fact."

With slow deliberation, Casey faced the door once more. She didn't say goodbye. She couldn't. She opened the door just wide enough to slip through and close it silently behind her. Then she stood, her back to the cold molding, and stared at the wall across from her. Her breathing was short and shallow. Her pulse raced and she felt a tingling flush on her skin.

Why? she wondered. Why did he have to tell her private things about her family that could hurt so much—things that could change the way she felt about the people in her life?

Casey swallowed back the lump in her throat. Damn him! He had no right to ask her here only to bombard her with bad feelings and an intense sadness about things that were never as she had wanted them to be.

She could understand that in some way he thought he was reaching out. He believed no one had heard his side of the story, old as it was, and he needed to try to explain to someone who cared. It was his only excuse for his own detached behavior.

She knew that feeling. She'd had it often enough, especially when it came to her father. She'd dreamed of confronting him and telling him off, then walking away with her head held high, knowing that he would suffer for the rest of his life for having heard the truth from her point of view.

Instead, she walked away in tears.

Matt's shadow flowed over her. "That was a short visit."

She looked up, and the blue of his uniform seemed as blue and stormy as she felt. His lightly-callused hands covered her arms, quickly rubbing to induce heat back into her. She saw the concern in his eyes, but she couldn't respond to it without bursting into tears. Instead, she ignored it.

"It was over before it began. I knew I shouldn't have come. I should have stayed in my own world where I was safe and happy, and let him continue in his."

"That's not true and you know it."

She stared up at him, knowing her eyes were still filled with tears but refusing to let them fall. "It is too. The man in that hospital room bears no resemblance to my idea of a father. He's just someone I knew as a kid."

"Give him a chance, Casey. He deserves that, at least," Matt urged.

But she couldn't do that. "Why? He never gave me one."

"You've come this far, Casey. Stick it out for the weekend. When it's over, if you still want to leave and never see him again, I'll help you cut those strings. But don't make a decision based on one short twenty-minute visit."

She closed her eyes and sighed. "Why in heaven's name am I beating myself up like this? I ought to get out of here as quickly as I can."

"Stay," he coaxed, a smile tilting his full lips. "I'll take you out to the River Walk for dinner and dancing tonight."

She returned his smile. "Who pays?"

"Me. I'll force myself to pay the entire tab and never bring it up." He raised a hand as if swearing an oath. "Scout's honor."

Knowing she needed to stay and confront a few of these new, unsteady emotions concerning her dad, Casey allowed herself to be persuaded. She glanced at her watch. "Can you tell me how to get to the Colonel's place and let me rest for a little while?"

"I'll do better than that," he answered huskily, his fingers still curled around her arms, lending her his warmth. "I'll escort you there. It's not far from my own town house."

"Okay. But I have to warn you. I might pull out of the driveway tomorrow morning and not return."

"Just give it some thought first, Casey. Don't do anything you might regret later, when it's too late to correct it."

"I don't make rash decisions, Major. But once I make up my mind, I usually stick to it." Just because she'd opted to stay for the night didn't guarantee that she'd visit the Colonel again.

Matt chuckled at her warning. "Like father like daughter," he murmured, continuing before she could protest. "Just give the Colonel some time. That's all I ask." He dropped his arms and she was surprised at how much she missed his warmth. "I'll meet you in the parking lot," he said, stepping around her and placing his broad, square hand on the door to push it open. "I know where you're parked."

Casey nodded, then quickly headed down the hall toward the elevators. She didn't want to see inside that room again. And she didn't want the Colonel to know that she'd been standing outside his door all this time. She refused to let him recognize just how upset she really was.

Taking her time walking to her truck, she looked around at all the people bustling through the parking area. Most wore military uniforms—a sight she hadn't seen in a long time. Even though San Antonio boasted five major bases and posts, there were no air or army installations in Houston.

At one time she had loved being a part of the military. She'd been a small child, then. By the time she'd entered fourth grade and was first learning to answer the phone, she'd found that more responsibility went to a military daughter than to her civilian friends.

Also, it was when she was old enough to answer the phones, the arguments between her parents began.

Like most military children at that time, she lived on base in officers' housing, but buses picked her up and took her to school in the city. By fourth grade she'd made friends who couldn't wait to get home and test their skills by telephoning everyone they knew in school. Casey was no exception.

During this period, her father had been absent for almost two weeks, and this was his first evening home. By dinnertime that night Casey had answered the phone four times and twice it had been for her. She'd felt so proud of her accomplishments....

"Guess what?" she said at the dinner table. "Two of my friends called me today."

"And Casey made two calls today, too," her mother interjected with a proud smile.

"Were your friends children of officers, Casey?" her father asked.

She frowned, trying to remember if they had mentioned anything about the military. "I don't know. Why?"

"Because little girls whose daddies are officers are supposed to play with other officers' children," her father stated brusquely.

Not sure why she was so embarrassed, Casey stared at her plate.

"I'm sure both her friends were civilian, honey," her mother said quietly.

"Did you answer the phone?" her father asked her.

Casey nodded. Her smile faded into the confusion of the conversation.

"What did you say?"

"I said, 'Hello.'"

Her father stared across at her mother. "You didn't teach her how to answer the phone?"

"She's still young, dear," her mother answered. "I'm sure that your commanding officer will understand if he calls and she hasn't quite got through phone-answering class 101."

Her father gave her mother a stern look laced with disgust, then turned his steel blue eyes on her. "If you're old enough to answer the phone, young lady, then you're old enough to answer it correctly."

Casey wasn't sure what she had done, but she knew she'd done something very, very wrong. Tears welled in her eyes as she stared up at the man she most wanted to please in the whole wide world. She was afraid to trust her voice. Instead, she bit her lip and nodded.

"When you answer the phone, you must say, 'Major Porter's quarters, this is Cassandra speaking.'" He waited a moment for it to sink in. "Do you understand?"

She didn't. But Casey nodded again.

"Say it," he demanded.

"Stanley," her mother protested.

Still pinning Cassandra to her seat with his intimidating gaze, he raised his hand in the air to motion her mother to silence. "Say it," he ordered.

"Major Porter's quarters. Casey talking."

"No," he said firmly. "Say it exactly the way I told you. Again."

"Stanley, that's enough badgering. She's just a child, for heaven's sake, not one of your enlisted men jumping all over themselves to please you."

"Unlike my family, they try to please and not thwart me at every turn."

"That's not true and you know it. Besides, perhaps you treat them better than your family."

Another skirmish between her parents began.

A few minutes later, Casey scooted off her seat and left the table, secure that her father would remember the next night and coach her again on the correct way to answer their phone. She was equally sure that her mother and father would fight for the rest of the night. Then, in the morning, her mother would begin patiently teaching her how to say the necessary words by rote....

Looking back, it had always been the same pattern—the same anger, the same frustration.

Casey was aware that her mother and father's relationship had always been under stress. A couple of years later, when they were living in Frankfurt, Germany, her mother took her back to the States for a visit. Although the word *separation* was never spoken, Casey knew she wouldn't see her dad again for a while. The truth was in her mother's eyes when she told Casey to kiss her father goodbye. And her father, usually so stiff in his dress uniform, had bent down and enfolded her in such a tight hug that for a moment, she didn't want to leave him.

"Be a good little soldier and mind your mother," he'd said gruffly as he stood and patted her on the head. Her sadness had suddenly changed to resentment. She wasn't their pet dog, Bowser, who was leaving. And she wasn't a soldier. She was his *daughter*.

Sighing heavily now, Casey wished she hadn't stirred up such sad memories. She climbed into her truck and turned on the air-conditioning while she waited for Matt. The sun was hotter than the breeze, and she rolled down her window to let out the baked air. After adjusting the vents, she leaned back and closed her eyes.

Earlier she'd promised herself that she wouldn't let this visit upset her. Yet, here she was, remembering things that she didn't want to remember, defending people that she didn't need to defend, feeling guilty over past actions that were never in her control. She felt like that little girl again—insecure, scared, always worried about never doing a good enough job.

A cool breeze touched her skin, then she felt the soft firmness of lips brush hers. A zing raced down her spine. She knew instantly that it had to be Matt. She opened her eyes.

His strong face was just inches from hers. "Did I wake you?"

"Yes."

"Does that mean we have to have a wedding now?"

Casey frowned. "What?"

"In fairy tales, if the prince wakens the princess with a kiss, he marries her and they live happily ever after," he explained patiently in his sexy, gravelly voice. He was trying to get a smile out of her, and she finally obliged.

She tried to ignore the tantalizing scent of him wafting through the window. "Lucky for you, I have some demanding dwarfs I have to take care of at home, so the marriage will have to wait until my next life."

"What a waste." His breath moved over her cheeks and mouth like a heated caress, calling every sense to attention. "And I had some free time."

"Mmm," was all she could manage before swallowing her emotions. It had already been a day fraught with highs and lows. She didn't need to add anything to it.

"Well then, if you won't marry me I'll lead you to the Colonel's town house. It's only a few doors down from mine," he said, pulling his head out of the interior of the truck. "Follow me."

She nodded. As she watched him walk away, she wondered if his buns were really as nice as they looked in that uniform. *Stop that!* she told herself. *Remember where you are and who you are with, and you won't get yourself in trouble!*

Getting involved with a military man was something she'd sworn never to do. Matt was off-limits. She knew that. She'd just forgotten for a minute.

Her father's town house was on the north side of San Antonio, toward Shavano Park, a prestigious area in the foothills of the Hill Country. The complex was hidden behind a redbrick wall strapped with blooming vines of lush, pink roses. The entrance, right down to the stained-glass half-moon above the door, reminded her of a cozy English cottage. But when Matt opened the door and stepped aside, she realized the image of coziness disappeared at the front door.

A utilitarian brown couch with matching chair looked dull against the contemporary gray carpet. It took a moment, but Casey recognized the coffee and end tables as the ones her parents owned when she was eleven. A TV with an outdated guide on it sat in the corner, looking like a one-eyed sentry.

"Dear, sweet heaven," she muttered, flipping on a light switch. The curtains were pulled closed but bright sunlight streamed through the fabric enough to show the dingy living area.

She walked into the hallway, then stopped at the master bedroom. Again, she saw furniture she remembered. This time, her parents' bedroom set, dusty and in need of polish, filled the space. But this room had a softer look. Several paintings relieved the bare, white walls. An intricately woven tapestry hung over the mahogany bed. All were well remembered and obviously treasured relics of the family's stay in Germany.

Matt came up behind her, standing just outside the bedroom door, his narrowed gaze taking in her emotional disturbance. "Are you all right?"

"As okay as I can be when I've just walked back into my past," she joked. Her voice shook.

"I guessed as much. I don't know the history of the furniture, but I had a feeling it was your parents'."

"It was. Only now it's the worse for wear."

"Think so?" Matt looked around. "I thought it was pretty solid stuff."

"You're military," she replied. "But take my word for it—'solid' doesn't have to be aesthetically pleasing."

"I'm male," he retorted dryly. "But, I would guess that in your book the answer would be the same for both afflictions."

"That, too," she said, grinning. It was her first genuine smile today. "But I trust you in spite of myself."

"Prove it. Stay at my house." She hesitated, and he continued. "There are too many memories here for you to be comfortable."

He was right and they both knew it. The emotional trauma of the day had exhausted her and she needed to rest. "Fine."

Without another word, they walked out the door and Matt carefully locked it behind them. Then, taking her elbow, he led her down the path toward the end of the row of town houses.

Casey wished she'd stayed home in Houston.

4

A SHARP SOUND WOKE Casey. The room was dim, she could only see the outlines of the heavy furniture. For a moment, she forgot where she was. Her gaze darted around the unfamiliar room, finally landing on the framed awards and plaques on the far wall of the bedroom/home-office. Then the past several hours came flooding back.

Matt had escorted her through his home, directly into the guest room. While her guard was down, he'd brushed another light, comforting kiss on her chilled mouth. As she was still wishing that the kiss had gone further, he'd left her, closing the door quietly behind him. After he'd disappeared, she wasn't sure if she felt overtired or just a deep regret that he was leaving instead of staying to share the double bed.

It hadn't mattered. Two minutes later, minus her shoes, jacket and shirt, Casey had fallen asleep. Her dreams had been of Matthew and the Colonel.

A glance at her watch told her it was almost five o'clock. The same noise that woke her filtered through the closed door again, only this time she recognized it—it was the hollow sound of a metal pot striking something. She hoped he wasn't cooking dinner. He'd promised her an evening on the downtown River Walk, and that's what she wanted. Seeing people doing things that were ordinary and fun would calm her nerves. Something good should come out of this weekend, and anything to do with people-watching in the fabulous, touristy restaurants and shops along the downtown San Antonio River sounded just like the answer.

Slipping into her skirt took only a minute. Her suitcase was still in her truck, so all she could do was rinse her mouth, brush her hair and freshen her makeup with what was available in her purse. Once finished, she slid into her pumps and headed toward the noise.

Matt stood with his back to her as he rinsed dishes and set them in a rack on the counter. Even from behind, he looked gorgeous. He was dressed in white tennis shorts and a matching sweater. White socks and running shoes completed the outfit. With his sun-streaked hair, he looked like the backside of an ad in a women's magazine for the sexiest man alive. And his buns were as shapely as she had guessed earlier.

"Has anyone ever taught you the virtues of a dishwasher?" she asked, entering the area and reaching around him for a glass on the drainer.

Glancing over his shoulder, he grinned endearingly. "Sure, but by the time I have enough dishes to fill it, the food will have caked into a hard crust that

not even steaming water from a dishwasher can elim-
inate."

"That sounds logical," she mused. "But it also
points out the fact that you don't cook much."

"I do fine," he corrected, then nodded his head in
the direction of the refrigerator. "Cold water's in
there."

She followed his direction and filled her glass. Sipping it, she leaned against the countertop as she stared
out the door leading to a narrow garden path. Lush
with flowers and bushes on either side of the flagstone, there was barely room to stroll the stone-
covered walkway to the gate. She was sure he chose
his plants for more than just their easy maintenance.
They had alternating flowering times, which meant
he'd have something in bloom all through the sum-
mer.

"Who designed your garden?"

"I did, through trial and error."

"It's beautiful."

Matt turned his intense gaze on her while slowly
and methodically wiping his hands on a dish towel.
"Coming from you, that's a high compliment, indeed."

"I mean it," she said. "You've done an excellent job
of balancing the florals with the bloomers."

His eyes were focused on her mouth. Nervously she
licked her lips to wet them and his gaze darkened sen-
suously. She felt every single move he made, every

reaction he had to her. It was sexual. Purely and simply. And it was obvious in the way they stood, touched, moved their mouths, eyes and hands. Their need for each other was so thick and hot, Casey could have sworn the air snapped and sizzled between them.

"Don't." She didn't know she'd uttered the word until she heard it.

His gaze darted to hers. "Why not?"

"It's wrong. *We're* wrong."

"So we are," he agreed in a low voice. His gaze once more fastened on her mouth, his eyes narrowing. "But that doesn't make this attraction any less."

Her pulse beat so rapidly it felt like champagne bubbles flowing through her veins. "There shouldn't *be* an attraction," she protested.

Matt's tawny-colored head nodded slowly. "I know. We're all wrong for each other."

"Right."

"But both of us feel the pull."

"Speak for yourself." She tried to pretend she didn't feel it. But it was no use. His presence overwhelmed her. He was the most handsome man she'd been this close to in a very long time. The strange thing was that she'd never been drawn to strictly handsome men before.

Why now? she wondered as she stared, fascinated by the flex of his mouth. She knew the reason. His kindness toward her when she'd needed it most had made all the difference in the world. His personality added to the intense physical attraction.

Matt cocked an intimidating brow. "Think we're both smart enough to stay out of emotional traps and not hurt each other's feelings?"

"Oh, I think so," she said dramatically, trying to tease herself out of a serious mood. "Just because I'm female doesn't make me overemotional. And just because you're military doesn't make you *completely* robotlike."

He frowned. "Are you attacking me so soon?"

She pulled away and smiled sweetly over her glass. "I don't know. Did I hit a nerve?"

He dropped the cloth and leaned on the counter, one hand on either side of her. His gray-eyed gaze delved much deeper than she cared to show or admit. Casey kept her smile even though she was sure it looked stiff. She didn't want him to know, but her breath was caught somewhere deep in her throat by the sheer masculinity of him.

He smiled in return, but it reminded her of a tiger stalking a tiny mouse. "Several nerves, but I don't think you want to hear about them all."

Again, she felt flustered. "As long as we understand that this—this . . ."

"This intense sexual attraction?" he supplied smoothly.

"This irresponsible fascination," she corrected in a breathy voice, "isn't good for either of us, and that we are certainly adult enough to keep it under control for the two weeks you're working for me."

"You're holding me to my offer, aren't you?"

It was her turn to look cool. "But of course. I wouldn't have taken off this weekend if I thought for a moment that you weren't going to uphold every part of our bargain."

He nodded. "Of course."

With one more enigmatic look, he pulled away and headed for the front door. She had to force herself not to haul him back to her. Reason won—for the moment.

"I'll be back after my run. Dress up, lady. We're painting the town," he said over his shoulder. "We can go to dinner right after I shower."

"That ought to be an interesting sight," she muttered under her breath as she watched him let himself out the front door. He obviously had a restaurant in mind. It wasn't until he was gone that she realized she hadn't asked him where they were eating so she knew what "Dress up" meant.

Her resolve stiffened. She was a grown woman in her middle years with two adolescent sons and a profitable business. She could figure out what to wear all by herself. In fact, it was about time she took charge of the situation. Since her arrival at the hospital, she hadn't been in control.

She grabbed her keys, then retrieved the overnight bag from the back seat of her truck. After finding the iron in the kitchen pantry, she gave her outfit a quick once-over.

Minutes later, she stood in the guest-bathroom shower with steaming water sluicing down her body. Aches and tensions from the day washed down the drain along with the soapy water. As the minutes passed, she felt more focused, her emotions under control.

Stepping out of the shower, she smiled smugly into the foggy mirror. She'd won the battle of mind over matter. Major Matthew Patterson was back in his proper place in her mind as an emissary of her father, a fellow co-worker and a kind—though military— man.

The front door opened, then closed, and Casey stiffened. Her much-vaunted control slipped when she heard the sound of water being turned on. For just a second, she imagined his lean, strong, naked body slipping behind the shower curtain and her pulse raced.

Determined to prove her control, she carefully applied her makeup and did her hair, then slipped into her strapless black sundress and matching bolero jacket. Low black heels completed the outfit. With a look in the mirror that confirmed she'd done her best with what she had, Casey walked down the hall to the living room.

She'd barely noticed the room when Matt had first led her through it. Now, as she looked around, Casey realized that it was well furnished with expensive contemporary pieces. But warmth—the color accents that usually tied a room together—was missing. There were no complementary colors to highlight the tans and browns. A painting on one wall, however, was a great, if unmatched, crayon-colored focal point. A watercolor of Southwest flavor hung across from it. She walked over and stared at the signature. Michael Atkinson. It was a beautiful piece—one that illuminated tall, pastel canyon cliffs against the pale blue of a desert sky.

"I bought that last year, when I visited his studio in Austin." Matt stood just inside the doorway in his blue uniform. He looked simply gorgeous. Casey turned back to the watercolor, unwilling to let him know how deeply he stirred her. "It's beautiful."

"So are you."

"Thank you." She turned her head and stared at him. "Why are you in uniform? I thought we were going out."

"We are, but I have to make a small detour. I'm supposed to show up at my new commanding officer's home for a drink. I promise it won't take more than fifteen minutes."

"That's what Dad used to say," Casey said.

"Only I mean it. I know how you feel about my job. Besides, I'm not too fond of these things myself."

Casey raised her brows. "But you trust me not to kick him in the shins or get drunk and embarrass you?"

"I'll take the chance." Matt sighed heavily. "Let's get out of here."

"Where to?" Casey asked, reaching for her purse. She was glad to be going out in public with him. Being together, alone, was difficult for her self-control.

"You'll see." He escorted her out the door, his hand resting firmly on the base of her spine, sending heat through the rest of her body. She tried to ignore it, but couldn't.

Moments later, they walked into his commanding officer's home, met his wife, two daughters and a few other guests. Most of them knew her father, or of him, so conversation was easy, drifting around his health problem and how he was dealing with it. Casey was surprised at how many of the guests knew about her. She hadn't realized that her father had spoken of her. It was a mixed feeling of pleasure and pain.

By the time Casey finished her drink, Matt apologized to the group and shepherded her out the door.

"That was quick," she commented.

"I thought it was best."

She didn't ask why. Casey didn't want to know.

As he'd promised earlier, Matt drove downtown, parking the car a short way from a well-known Mexican restaurant on the River Walk. But he led her instead to the deck of a flat-bottomed boat where several other diners were already seated at the pristine, linen-covered tables.

"We're eating on board?" she asked, a smile lighting her eyes as well as her heart.

"I gather you like the idea."

"I love it. But why? How?"

His own answering grin showed just how pleased her excitement made him. "I made the reservations when you were sleeping. I decided that if we were coming down here, we might as well do it the fun way. Besides, the mosquitos can't get a grip on a moving target."

Matt's wit and Casey's laughter set the mood for the evening. Dinner was delicious, the wine delightful, the waiters discreet. The others on the boat added to the lighthearted party atmosphere. Two hours later, Casey and Matt stepped off the boat and meandered down the sidewalk past the River Walk bars and restaurants. A small jazz place with a piano practically next to the water drew them in. They ordered after-dinner drinks and listened to the sounds of sweet jazz from a trio known for their innovative tunes.

It was past midnight before they headed toward the parking lot. Matt caught and held her hand as they strolled alongside the bank of the San Antonio River. She felt so content. Shouldn't that be a warning sign? But she was too content to let it matter.

Music drifting from open club doors competed with the chatter of revelers moving from one night spot to the next. Delicious aromas from various restaurants wafted together, making a wonderful potpourri of fragrances that the River Walk claimed exclusively as its own.

Leaving the colorful lights behind them, they took the stone staircase to the street level and walked silently to the car. As Matt slipped the key in the ignition, Casey leaned back and sighed deeply.

"Talk to me. What's going on in that lightning-quick mind of yours?" Matt asked.

She gave him a lazy smile, noticing his eyes crinkle as he smiled back. "It was a wonderful evening. Thank you. I'm the most relaxed I've been in a million years."

"You don't relax much, do you?" he asked, his voice as thick and dark as the Kahlúa she'd had with her after-dinner coffee.

"I don't have time. There's always something to be done or to get ready to do."

"You're too young to be so tied down and tired out from running a business."

She smiled again. "I love what I do. It's just that it isn't easy being mother and father to two growing boys, then trying to give everything you've got to your own business."

He raised a brow in question. "And sometimes it's more tiring than others?"

In the half shadow of the car, she caught her breath at the sight of the devastatingly masculine man beside her. He seemed to have this effect on her whenever he was close. "I'm just sorry the evening is over."

"It's not. I have a cappuccino machine at home that's just waiting for us. Along with it, there's a rich liqueur you might like."

"My, my. You sound prepared for everything." She didn't mean for her jealousy to show, but she felt it. He was a bachelor. How many other women did he offer his hospitality to? She didn't want to know. She did, too, a small voice argued.

"Why? Because I enjoy cappuccino and liqueur? Would you believe—" he leaned closer to her ear, his warm breath a whisper "—I even drink it occasionally when I'm alone?"

"Really? I can't imagine you by yourself too often." Her voice was sharp.

He hesitated only a moment before he dropped all the teasing and spoke plainly. "There was a time in my life when I wasn't alone much. Almost every night there was a woman in my house—at my table or in my bed. But nothing lasts forever without change. I had to face the fact that despite my busy life I still wasn't content."

"Why?"

"Because, happiness comes from within. Not from a great sex life."

"I'm surprised you haven't found someone you could be compatible with."

Matt pulled into his driveway, reached up and pushed the button for the automatic garage-door opener. When it opened completely, he pulled into the dimly lit interior and killed the engine.

The silence between them spoke almost as loudly as words. Tension was rife, yet neither was willing to end it by making a move toward their car door.

Finally, Matt turned toward her, the light so dim all she could see was his outline and the glistening depths of his eyes. "Casey? Let's call a truce."

"I didn't know we were fighting."

"Yes, you did." He refused to allow her to hide behind words. "But let's be friends. Maybe even allies for a little while. Things will get done quicker and work smoother if we stop dodging the obvious."

"You're talking about *us* again." It was a statement.

"Yes."

"What exactly do you mean by 'truce'?"

"Let's go inside, put on some coffee, listen to some music and enjoy each other's company. It's what we both want to do, anyway. I'm not going to seduce you."

Casey felt put in her place. She reached for the door handle and opened the car door. "Don't worry. I wouldn't let you get far."

Matt opened his door and stepped out, then waited for her to come around before they walked into the house. Just as she reached his side, the timed, automatic-door light clicked off. Blackness surrounded them. For just a moment, Casey felt a touch of panic. Then his warm hand encased her waist and pulled her close to him, so that her breast touched his hard, broad chest.

"Are you okay?" he asked, his voice sounding huskier in the darkness.

She cleared her throat. Hot fire sizzled down her spine, but she quelled it. In a no-nonsense tone she answered, "I'm fine. Are we going in the house or staying in the dark?"

His chuckle wafted on the dark air. "Don't worry, Casey. I'm not going to attack you here, either."

"I never thought you would."

"Yes, you did," he contradicted calmly, leading her toward the kitchen door. "Rest assured that if and when we ever make love, we'll be somewhere I can see your face."

"Don't get too cocky, Major," she warned, disguising a sigh of relief as he opened the door and light flooded them. He was wrong. She'd been afraid of seduction, not force. She didn't stand a chance of warding him off—she wanted him too much.

His hand drifted away from her waist and she missed his touch just as much as she was relieved by its absence.

Matt went directly to the cappuccino machine on the counter and began making the brew. Good, she thought, somewhat miffed that she could so wholeheartedly respond to someone who didn't seem to have any reaction to her.

She scooted around the doorway and went directly to her bathroom. One glance in the mirror told her she looked as if she'd spent a windy time on the boat; her hair was disheveled, curling in wild abandon. Her lipstick was gone, as was any mascara she might have applied that afternoon. Reaching into her purse, Casey began repairing her makeup.

By the time she returned to the kitchen, Matt had put on the CD player and the strains of a slow, easy ballad from the Big Band era filled the town house.

"Coffee's done," he said with a smile as he surveyed her.

She reached for the clear glass cup he handed her and blushed, wishing she hadn't retouched her makeup. Not knowing what to say that wouldn't give away her feelings, Casey turned her back and pretended to study a grouping of paintings and framed prints on the wall.

Matt came up behind her and her every nerve tensed. His warm breath caressed the back of her neck and cheek. Refusing to acknowledge him, she sipped her drink and continued to look at the artwork.

"What's going on, Casey?" he finally asked.

Without turning around, she questioned him. "What do you mean?"

"I mean all the mixed signals you keep giving me."

Her chin tilted defiantly. "Don't flatter yourself, Major. I'm not sending any signals at all."

"Don't lie, Casey. You've always been straightforward with me, even when it hurt. Now isn't the time to hold back."

She turned, anger apparent in her expression. "Thank you for your assessment of my character, Major, but I didn't ask for it. I know exactly what I'm doing and saying, and I don't need you to interpret my actions."

"If you weren't trying to draw my attention, why put on fresh makeup when we've returned from an evening out? Why not scrub your face clean and go to bed?"

Damn him! She felt a blush sweep from her neck to her forehead. "I didn't put on makeup for you."

"Oh." He grinned knowingly. "You put it on for someone else?"

She tilted her chin. "Yes. Me."

Matt's grin changed, turning tender and caring. "Then I apologize for jumping to conclusions."

Setting her cup on the table, Casey smiled sweetly. "Major? Go to hell." With one graceful movement, she swept out of the living room and down the hall to her room.

The Major's husky laugh followed close behind her.

5

CASEY TOSSED AND TURNED in the dark. Every time she drifted into slumber, her dreams were filled with erotic images. Then she'd wake up, toss some more, and drift back into a light sleep.

Major Matt was to blame for the entire thing. For her lack of sleep, her tension-filled day with her father—and especially for her unusual lack of calm.

Around four in the morning she gave up trying to sleep. Slipping on her lightweight robe, she carefully tiptoed down the hall and into the kitchen. She filled the kettle and turned on the electric burner, then searched in the refrigerator for a lemon. Instead, she found bottled lemon juice.

"A man's pantry," she muttered, reaching for a cup and filling the bottom with the yellow juice.

"Don't women use juice in a bottle?" Matt asked from the doorway.

Casey jumped. He was leaning against the jamb, wearing nothing but a towel around his hips. His shoulders and chest glistened with droplets of water. His skin was the color of gold and copper.

She stared straight at him, totally in control. "You owe me an apology."

His smile slipped as he turned serious. "You're right. I behaved terribly." He frowned. "My only defense is that when I'm with you, I do and say things I normally wouldn't say or do. I'm not sure I understand it, but I become a little crazy when you're around."

Casey slowly smiled. She knew that feeling herself. Intimately. She let down her guard a little.

"Our opinions aren't the same, but we should be adult enough to work around that. You and I will be working together for two weeks and then we're both free to lead our own lives again. Let's see if we can make being around each other tolerable."

"That's only half the problem," he stated wryly. "'Tolerable' isn't how I'd describe being around you."

She decided to ignore that comment as well as her racing heart. The kettle steamed and she pulled it off the burner, then poured hot water into her cup. "What are you doing up? I thought military people were supposed to sleep through world wars so they wouldn't miss roster the next morning." She squirted some extra lemon juice into her hot water.

"I couldn't sleep either, so I decided to take a cold shower," he stated, laughter tingeing his voice. "It's good to know I wasn't the only one having a restless night—that the cool-and-collected Cassandra Porter Lund occasionally gets her own feathers ruffled."

She turned and leaned against the counter, crossed her arms and sipped the hot liquid as if she'd had the most restful sleep in the world. "I wouldn't bet on it."

"You mean you always rise at five in the morning?" he asked. "My, my, the military did train you well."

Her chin tilted defiantly. "Don't push me, Major, or I might bite back."

Matt moved toward her and reached for a glass from the cabinet behind her. He was so close, his body brushed against her. "Don't I wish you would. Anything would be better than the pain you've already inflicted." His tone was low, suggestive and sexy as hell.

She felt a flush start in her face and course all the way down her body to her curling toes. Her gaze darted up to lock with his and her breath caught in her throat. Matt's need was as hot and pulsing and palpable as hers, and it shone like a beacon in a storm from the gray of his eyes.

His gaze dropped to her neck. "I can see your pulse beating in the hollow of your throat," he said thickly.

She couldn't think. With a slowness that rivaled eternity Matt bent his head and placed a light kiss on that spot. Her pulse raced and she moaned.

"Tell me," he coaxed. "I have to hear you, Casey. Tell me I'm not alone with these crazy feelings. Tell me you want me as much as I want you."

His mouth made contact with her skin again and she gasped out, "Yes."

"Tell me we should do something about it."

Casey was afraid to nod. Her feelings were so chaotic she clenched the cup until her fingers went numb.

"Tell me, dammit."

"I want you," she finally managed, her voice hardly above a soft murmur.

Matt's hand covered hers, silently telling her he wanted the cup she held. But her fingers didn't want to loosen their hold. He took a step back. "Are you really attached to that mug or are you thinking of using it as a weapon?"

"No, I..." she began, and her fingers finally moved, the cup spilling its now warm contents down her robe to her bare feet. She glanced down, her mind running in as many directions as the water she'd splashed.

Matt didn't blink an eye. With one hand he rescued the cup and set it on the countertop. The other hand reached for the towel that circled his hips. He flicked it off and pressed the terry-cloth fabric against her damp robe.

Casey ignored his movements. Matt stood calmly, completely naked, in front of her. He'd already declared his need aloud, and now his body confirmed his words.

Her own wants, so strong they heated her blood to boiling, finally overwhelmed her. Her hand covered his, stopping his movement and pressing his hand to her belly.

"Please," she whispered when he looked into her eyes.

"Yes." Relief echoed through his voice. One small word that meant so much.

Taking her hand in his, Matt led her down the hall to his bedroom, then to his bed. His hands, far more sure than hers, untied the flimsy robe and pushed it off her shoulders.

She felt the night air chill her skin, but not for long. Matt's mouth skimmed her neck as he undid the buttons on her pajama top and slipped it down from her shoulders.

"Oh, my," she whispered throatily as she watched his expression change from lust to tenderness.

"All mine," he corrected teasingly. Taking her breasts in his hands, he tilted her nipples toward his mouth.

His mouth was like warm lightning on her skin. Her breath hissed at his first touch. But it was more than his touch that stroked the core of her. He touched her mind.

For years she'd been mother, daughter, businesswoman. Now Matt made her feel feminine and desirable. As new as the feeling was, it was also deliciously wicked and wonderful.

Dizzy, she held on to his broad shoulders. Her eyes closed and the world shrank until it was just them. She reveled in his touch. It was the only thing in her world.

When he picked her up and placed her on the rumpled sheets of his bed, she was engulfed by the scent of him. It made her more light-headed than the most expensive champagne could. He stripped her of her pajama bottoms and stretched out next to her, his hands stroking back her hair as he gazed into the depths of her eyes.

Moonlight filtered through the partially open window just enough to illuminate his features. "Look at me, Casey. It's me, Matt."

She smiled, outlining his stern mouth with her fingertip until it softened. "I know who you are."

"I just want to make sure. I don't want any ghosts between us."

"It's you I want," she said softly.

He kissed her so tenderly it brought tears to her eyes. She wrapped her arms around him and silently thanked the powers that be for bringing him into her life before she forgot how wonderful it was to share intimacy with a man.

Not just any man. Matt.

All cohesive thoughts fled as he caressed her body, breast to thigh. Sighs collected in the air. Lips sought lips and limbs entwined.

Suddenly Matt pulled away and Casey felt bereft. She heard the drawer of his nightstand open and shut. "Matt?"

Then he was back, his kisses touching her cheek and eyes. "It's okay," he murmured. "I just had to be prepared, honey."

Her mind didn't grasp what his words were saying. "Prepared for what?"

"For making love to your beautiful body." There was a deep chuckle in his voice.

"I haven't been with anyone."

"But over the past years, I have. I don't want any regrets over our actions tomorrow or next week or next month, Casey. I want you to have only good memories. This way, I ensure that you won't worry about my partners or your periods."

She felt a blush creep up her face at the bluntness of his words, but she was also very relieved. She hadn't been thinking. Not at all.

"Thank you," she whispered before his mouth took command.

Seconds later, he entered her, and their rhythms matched, accentuating the flood of sensations arcing between them. Heat spiraled through Casey as she felt the heavens open to welcome her into the cocooning, velvety darkness that was punctuated by brilliant diamonds for stars.

Matt stiffened, his body warm and hard as a moan escaped his lips. Then, with a sigh, he rested against her. They both fought for breath and Casey marveled at the feeling of well-being that swamped her.

She didn't want to let go of him. She was afraid that once the connection was broken, the spell would end.

"Oh, Casey," he growled gently. "Whatever we did, it was the best I've ever felt."

Her laugh rivaled the moonlight, running down his spine like silver liquid. "What a nice thing to say."

He felt her putting up her walls again. Damn! It had taken him all this time to knock them down! Truth could be his only weapon. "It isn't nice, it's the truth. Don't you know how wonderful you are?" His tone was intimate. It did the trick. Her barriers fell.

Again she laughed. "In bed? No, I don't think I've been described as wonderful since my honeymoon," she said, a happy lilt in her voice that made him feel even better than great.

Matt shifted to the side and leaned on one arm so he could look down at her. "Hasn't there been anyone since your husband?"

She stared at his chest, her expression not quite so happy. "One. It was a mistake."

"On whose part?" he teased, trying to ignore the flash of jealousy that jolted him.

A grin peeped out as a reward. "Most of all, it was mine. I wasn't ready for an affair, but I was so . . ."

"Lonely?" he prompted.

"No." She shook her head for emphasis. Then her voice became hesitant at the memory. "I was so hungry to be touched. It was two years after Jerry died and I had felt so very alone for a human touch that soothed me, instead of the other way around. I just forgot that something else was needed to make it worthwhile."

"What was that?"

"Mutual caring and respect."

"Does that mean you care for me?"

Her body stiffened in response to his question. Immediately, he could tell he'd said the wrong thing. Unwilling to let these precious moments end, he quickly backtracked. "Or at least that you respect my decision to do what I do?"

She relaxed a little, but he could tell she was still wary. "Of course. I even respect what my father does. It just doesn't seem to be a two-way street, that's all."

He should have known better than to get into this conversation now, but he had to know how Casey felt about him. "With me or the Colonel?"

Casey sighed. "My father thinks everyone should worship the military. I don't. In fact, I respect his choice, but he doesn't respect my choices."

"Casey," Matt began, a warning in his voice.

Casey sat up, away from the warmth of his body. It was too tempting to let her emotions be swayed, and this was one subject she needed to clarify. "No, listen to me, Matt. Please. Just listen for a change."

He looked as if he was going to say something, then stopped. Plumping the pillows and leaning against the headboard, he crossed his arms on his chest. "Okay. No interruptions—for now. But I get the same chance later."

"Fair enough," she agreed. Sitting on her knees, Casey leaned toward him in her earnestness. "When I was growing up, my father was cold and distant. No matter what I did, he never warmed toward me. I was never given his attention unless I was very good or very bad. If I did well, I was his 'little soldier,' and if I did something wrong, I was a hindrance to his next promotion. And it always seemed that he wished I'd been a boy."

She could see he wanted to interject, but, true to his word, he remained silent. "It wasn't until after Mom and I left my father and lived away from the military for a while that I realized how depressed I'd become.

"Then Pops came into our life and with him came laughter and joy. For years, I missed my father, but when he finally decided to show up—at his convenience—I realized that I'd been wrong. I didn't miss him—I missed what I wished he'd been. I missed my idealized version of what a father should be. And I already had that in Pops."

She hesitated a moment, blinking away the tears that came with all the old memories. "I realized I was loved by someone else whose opinion was even more important—a man who loved me even though I wasn't his natural daughter. That made me worth something, Matt. Pops made me look at myself with esteem and pride. Not the Colonel. Pops."

Casey's earnestness made Matt realize just how hard it had been for her, growing up. He felt it to the very core and wished there was some way he could erase her hurt. But all he could do was marvel at Casey's ability to survive, to become the strong, beautiful woman she was.

When he finally spoke, he chose his words carefully. "You must have loved your father very much."

Her eyes were like liquid blue pools, and they showed her very vulnerable soul. "Yes." Her answer was simple. Honest. Heartbreaking.

"Don't you think it's time to come to terms with the past?"

"I already have."

Matt outlined her cheek with his finger. "But your father hasn't. And he has less time than any of us to do so."

Her smile was so sad it broke his heart. "The past five years and the loss of two people I dearly loved taught me that none of us have as much time as we would like to think, Matt."

His thumb lingered on the full curve of her mouth. "Give him a chance, Casey. For both your sakes."

Her brows rose languidly. "A chance for what?"

"Go back today. See him again. Find out if your ideas really do hold water."

Matt could see the thoughts and emotions crossing her face as she debated his words. She made her decision. "I will." But when he smiled, she held up her hand in order to stop his optimism. "But I'm leaving right after that. I have a living to earn and sons to raise."

"I know, I know. And that's fine. I just don't want you to regret anything about this visit. Including not following through on getting to know your father."

"I know my father very well," she stated firmly. "I've known him all my life and my opinion hasn't changed. Everything is the same, including our relationship."

"He's no ogre."

He longed to hold her close again, to lose himself inside her. She looked so soft, so sweet, so very vulnerable. But he knew this wasn't the time. Casey was too emotionally wound up.

She tilted her head and her mahogany hair spilled over her shoulders—dark satin against creamy skin. "I'll give him that, Matt. I'm not an ogre, either." She smiled slowly. "Besides, he has you as a friend and champion, so he can't be all bad."

"He has you for a daughter. You happened into a loving marriage, Casey. Don't downgrade that. Your father loved your mother, married her and wanted to have you. No matter how old he becomes or if he dies tomorrow, you can't rewrite that part of your history. Give him credit."

She pulled away and stood, wrapping the blanket around her like a form-fitting toga, then turned to leave. Matt felt as if he'd lost something special. He wanted to call her back, to ask her to stay and make love with him one more time. But he didn't.

At the door, Casey looked over her shoulder, unwittingly provocative enough for him to barely stifle a moan of need. "I guess I have to give you credit, too," she said quietly, a small smile playing seductively around her mouth. "Thank you."

"For talking about your father or for making love?"

A light blush tinged her skin, but her gaze never wavered. "For both, of course."

The end of the blanket swished across the carpet as she disappeared. Matt let out a sigh. Telling his body to relax didn't do much good. He was almost as tight and hard as just before he'd made love to Casey.

Snap out of it, man! he told himself. *This is the Colonel's daughter and you promised him you'd take care of her, not take her to bed!* He knew all that, but it didn't seem to make an impression where Casey was concerned. Her presence had an effect that overrode common sense.

It had to stop. They'd gone to bed once; it could end there. He'd get dressed, take her to the hospital to visit the Colonel and then he'd wave goodbye. He'd find someone else to work with her for two weeks. Temptation would then be removed.

Resolved, Matt jumped out of bed and into the shower—a very cold shower. Mind over matter wasn't quite as painless as it sounded.

WHEN CASEY WALKED INTO her father's hospital room, he was shaved, bright eyed and sitting up. "I've been waiting for you," he said, with a look that resembled relief in his eyes.

"Sorry. I overslept," she answered, taking a seat in the straight-backed chair next to his bed. She ignored Matt, who was standing behind her. "You look like you're doing much better."

"They tell me I can go home in a week."

"That's wonderful! I bet you'll be glad to get out of here," Casey said, meaning it. Even her father's lonely apartment couldn't be as depressing as a hospital.

"I can't go home unless there's someone to watch me—just to keep a check on my progress." He seemed reluctant—and sad—to give that information.

His gaze darted to Matt, and Casey thought she understood. "But then, you won't have to worry about that. Matt lives just around the corner. I'm sure he wouldn't mind keeping tabs on you."

Again, her father's eyes met Matt's. Feeling suspiciously like the odd man out of some well-kept secret, Casey looked at Matt, too.

He shrugged in puzzlement.

"I came up with a better idea, Cassandra," her father finally said. "One that I'm hoping you'll help with."

"If I can. Tell me what it is."

The Colonel reached out his hand and she clasped it in hers, hoping she was giving him strength. She didn't know what was on his mind, but it was obvious that he needed her. A warm feeling went through her. Perhaps, just perhaps, he did love her.

"I want to come stay at your house and recuperate. I could have a crew come in, fix up and add appliances to the garage apartment you have, and live there. Then, as soon as I'm well again, you'll have an apartment fit to rent out for more income."

"Stay with me? In the apartment?" She parroted his words, hardly believing he'd said them. "In Houston?"

"Yes," he said solemnly. "Fix up the apartment and stay with you for a little while. It would give me a chance to get to know my grandsons and I wouldn't be completely alone. Besides, the finished and furnished apartment would be a gift from me to you, so that you won't be out either your privacy or your money."

"How did you know about the apartment?" she asked. All those warm and daughterly feelings she'd had just a moment ago had vanished.

"I asked Matt and he told me there was a garage apartment, but that it looked as if it was used for storage."

She stared up at Matt accusingly. "Were you snooping, Major?"

"No, I just happened to notice that there were no curtains on the windows and could see boxes piled up inside."

"But—" she began again, wondering what excuse she could give for not wanting her own father there. She couldn't think of a thing. Well, perhaps one good reason. "But you and Pops wouldn't get along at all. You'd be better off here, with all your friends, and the military and all," she finished lamely.

"No. I'd be best off getting to know my grandsons and recuperating with family." Her father squeezed her hand, his expression turning sad. "You don't want me in your home, do you?"

"That's not it at all."

"Then what is it?"

Being tactful wasn't getting her anywhere. She might as well be blunt. "Look, Dad, I have a business and two children to raise. I work ten to twelve hours almost every day. I won't be around to watch you. The boys are too young. Pops already has his hands full. Besides, Pops is very important to me. I won't have him upset." She steeled herself for his reaction to her next statement. "Not even for you."

The older man looked offended. "I see. And you don't think I have the sense to know all that already? I'll have a nurse visiting every three or four days for the first two weeks. Stairs are good exercise for me. I'm an organized, disciplined man who can take care of himself. All I need is a little backup." His tone softened just enough to put a dent in Casey's heart. "I want a chance to get to know you, Cassandra. I feel as if I've been robbed of your growing years. I don't want to lose my grandsons' growing years, too."

That won her. "I don't think the apartment can be made ready in a week," she protested weakly.

Her father smiled for the first time since she'd entered the room. "You just leave that to me. I'll have a crew out there tomorrow."

Casey barely managed to return her father's smile. Why did she have a feeling she was in the middle of the ocean in a rowboat and there was a storm brewing?

Probably because she was.

6

WHEN CASEY LEFT HER father's hospital room, Matt was behind her. Anger rolled off her in thick, cold waves, chilling him in every nerve center. There was going to be hell to pay. Grimly, he followed her to the elevator.

They stepped on and the doors closed. Ignoring the young orderly with a cart loaded with supplies, Casey turned to face him. "Just tell me, Major. Was this your brainchild or were you only told a little sooner than I was?"

"I don't expect you to believe me, but I had no idea," he said honestly. "He'd asked me about where you lived and what the house and grounds were like, and I told him."

She stared into his eyes, her own still blazing hot with frustrated anger. "Okay, okay," she replied, taking a deep breath to calm herself. "I just didn't see this one coming. I should have, but I didn't."

"You're not alone. This was a surprise to me, too."

Her look told him she didn't quite believe that one. Even if it was true. For his sake, and with a deep-seated need he wouldn't look too closely into right now, he wanted her to trust him as he had never been trusted before.

"Look, I don't need to add to your problems right now," Matt said, halting only when the elevator doors opened. Casey exited, her heels clicking defiantly on the tile floor as she continued out the wide hospital doors and toward the car. "I'll find someone else to work with you for a couple of weeks."

"Work *for* me." She stopped in the middle of the parking lot, hand on her hip. "And, you'll do no such thing."

"Don't worry," he assured. "Whoever I choose, he'll be responsible and a hard worker. I'll handpick him myself."

"The hell you will, Major." She was still implacable. "You offered to work, and you will. That was the deal. No substitutions."

"I think we'd do better if we weren't in close quarters right now," he persisted. "Maybe later—"

"I don't care what you think. Our deal was that you would work for me for two weeks if I visited the Colonel. I'm sorry if you're having second thoughts because you went to bed with me, but you still owe me. You're coming to Houston. To work." Her tone was grim, her gaze like steel.

"Why?"

"Because, Major, you crashed into my life, sweet-talked me into coming here and reconciling with my father. You changed my whole way of living, upset my family and rearranged my priorities. Now I'm up to my ears in fathers, business and trouble. The least you can do is be around to help keep the Colonel and Pops from slitting each other's throats and make sure that my business doesn't fall apart under the strain of it."

"Thanks for the compliment," Matt stated dryly, feeling more responsible for her problems than he wanted to admit. "Fine. I'll be there."

"Great." Casey turned and walked off.

Matt stood, waiting for her to recognize the obvious. When she didn't, he finally yelled out, "Where are you going?"

"Home!" she shouted over her shoulder, her heels clicking again and her hips swaying enticingly.

"Are you going to walk there?"

She stopped, turned around and faced him from the other end of the parking aisle. If she wasn't wearing a suit and heels and if this wasn't the nineties, he would think they were at the O.K. Corral ready for a gunfight.

A resigned little sigh escaped her. "Right. We're in your Corvette."

Her truck was in front of his house, packed and ready to go back to Houston. He pointed to the shiny red car just a few spaces away. "And it's over there."

Once in the car, Matt stared at the steering wheel and tried to think of something to say that would reduce the tension. He couldn't think of a thing. Obviously, her anger was too strong for her to break the silence.

When they reached his town house, Matt pulled up behind Casey's truck.

"I wish I'd seen this coming, Casey. Maybe I could have deflected your dad. I know it's not going to be easy on you."

For the first time since he'd met her, Matt watched Casey slowly deflate. Soon all her anger was gone, leaving behind the sad taste of defeat. "It's not your fault. I'll manage." Then she sat up, straightening her spine. "Just be at my place in two weeks."

Matt's hand shot out and stopped her from leaving the car. "Are you sorry about last night?"

She smiled slowly, and it felt as if dawn were breaking. "No," she said softly. "No, I'm not sorry for that, Matt." Without another word, she leaned forward and placed a chaste kiss on his cheek.

But Matt wanted more. Tightening his hand and pulling her closer, he covered her mouth with his own. His need, as great now as it had been earlier that morning, surged through him. He felt his body adjust, shift, ready itself to make love to the woman in his arms and knew he had to pull away or pay the consequences. Part of him said to hell with consequences. She'd be gone soon enough from his life.

Her mouth was moist and warm and sent heat directly to the pit of his stomach. The scent of her hair surrounded him, making him think of flowers in springtime and lying in a field of clover—with her. He wanted to hold on to her, to keep her with him, under his heart. At least for an hour, a day. Maybe through the entire night. If he did so, instead of whetting his appetite for more of her, he might appease it in the warmth of her embrace.

"Casey," he murmured, spreading kisses over her cheeks and eyes. "Stay with me. One more day, Casey. One more day."

Her hands rested on his shoulders, her face tilted up like a flower to the sun. "I can't." She shook her head as if to emphasize her response. "I can't."

Matt sighed his resignation. He'd been hoping that something had changed and that she'd want to stay with him as much as he wanted to be with her. He should have known better.

As if she read his mind, her eyes clouded with the truth. "We'd never make it together."

"I know."

"We're from two different worlds, and I don't think I could ever live in yours. I'm not sure you could live in mine, either."

His tone was underlined with resignation. "I know."

"So can we just enjoy each other for the short time we'll be together and worry about the rest later?"

"I guess."

"But nothing can interfere with my family, Matt. Not my father. Not the military." Her voice lowered. "Not even you."

Matt's hands tightened on her arms, then he let go. "I know. You already set the ground rules when you said the same thing to your father."

Reluctance hung heavily in the air. Finally Casey pulled back and opened the car door. "I'll see you in two weeks?"

"Two weeks," he promised.

Casey stepped away from the curb and walked directly to her truck. She slipped behind the steering wheel, fumbled for her keys, started the engine and drove away. She never even looked in her rearview mirror.

Matt watched until the truck turned the corner and disappeared. When he reached his own back garden, he sat in his favorite chair and stared at the peach-and-pink-colored florals that bloomed there. She'd appreciated his work here. She'd appreciated and understood the tranquillity and sense of fulfillment that a well-tended garden—and home—could give its owner.

All Casey's traits and beliefs starkly contrasted with the quality of his own life before the military had given him calm and order. It was something he tried hard not to think about.

Most of the values and personal qualities she took for granted had been missing from his own life. Exemplars of which he had craved as a child growing up; character traits he had tried to cultivate in himself as a young man and, as a leader, had impressed upon the troops under him.

He'd grown up with just himself as his guide and guardian until he joined the air force at age seventeen. As he was growing up his aunt had alternately screamed at him or ignored him. He learned how to be on his own, but the rest was learned the hard way—by others' intolerance. He wasn't dumb. Then, when he joined the military he finally found a set of rules that made sense. And the man and the organization that had taught him, and whose values he respected the most, were the very ones Casey didn't want anything to do with.

The military. Her father.

He cursed under his breath. He'd known yesterday that he was fighting a losing battle. He'd also known she was right and that they came from two different worlds. So why was it so hard to admit that she didn't belong in his life?

The answer came to him in a slow-moving wave. For the first time in his life, he was falling in love—falling in love with the wrong woman for him. "Way to go, Major," he growled under his breath, using Casey's nickname for him.

He'd stop it. Mind Over Matter—wasn't that what the military taught? There was no obstacle one couldn't overcome if the cause was right and just. And he had too much common sense to want to be hurt by Casey. He was a survivor.

The Colonel had asked him to look out for Casey and he could do that. But the Colonel had also given veiled warnings about hurting Casey in any way. Matt had no doubt that falling in love with the woman wasn't going to make the Colonel a happy man.

He got up and went through the house to his bedroom. Without a thought to his clothes, he lay down on his bed, crossed his arms behind his head and stared at the ceiling. Casey's feminine scent clung to the sheets and pillow, enveloping him like invisible smoke.

With a precision he usually reserved for his work, he relived every single moment and movement of making love to Casey. This wasn't the end of their relationship—not yet. He promised himself he would hold her again. Somehow, some way, he'd make love to her again. It would make parting harder when the time came to end things, but they would both carry away some wonderful memories.

He had no doubt they would eventually part. Sooner or later they would tire of each other and each would go their own way. He simply wasn't a "forever" kind of guy. In all his relationships, after a while, he found he needed distance. In time, Casey would probably feel the same way. But they could enjoy each other *now*.

That thought was sweet torture.

THE DAY AFTER CASEY returned home, a five-man crew arrived to clean out the apartment she'd used as a storeroom. For the next five days, they painted, caulked, carpeted, rebuilt a kitchen area, fixed the long-unused plumbing and put up a wall to form a small bedroom off the living area. Finally they installed appliances and light fixtures, and brought in furniture.

Her father was supposed to arrive sometime tomorrow. Which meant she had the weekend to get her father settled in his new—and temporary—home. Pops had ignored the renovation proceedings, never mentioning a word to Casey about the crew, the mess, the furniture or the trucks that constantly blocked the driveway. Even when she'd told him about her father's visit, he'd never said a word.

Jeremy and Jason, however, were delighted with the unexpected activity. It broke up their routine and gave them something to look forward to. They had a million questions about a grandfather they'd never met, and Casey knew those questions put as much a strain on Pops as it did on herself. Because the Colonel was a novelty, he was getting more attention than Pops.

Now the apartment was finished and Casey wanted to look it over. As she started up the outside flight of stairs, she heard her neighbor calling, "Casey! Wait up!" Sara ran across her lawn to the steps. Sara, a widow much closer to Pops's age than hers, was one of Casey's best friends.

"I've been waiting all week to see this transformation," she huffed as she caught up with Casey. "I'm not going to miss it now."

"You've seen all the hubbub." Casey opened the door and stood back. "Welcome to the transformation."

Sara stepped inside and Casey came in behind her. Both of them stopped dead in their tracks. Champagne-colored carpeting covered every inch of space except for a small, tiled rectangle in the corner for the kitchen. The walls were painted golden with crisp white molding.

Sara whistled through her teeth. "How long did you say he was going to visit?"

"A couple of weeks," Casey said, wondering if she was being optimistic. "A month at most."

"I'm not sure, honey, but I'd call this apartment a permanent home. I don't know any man who would spend this much money for a couple of weeks' comfort." She crossed the carpet as if walking on eggs. Looking into the bedroom, her eyes widened again. "Even for a *year's* worth of comfort. This is really nice. Who was the decorator?"

"I have no idea," Casey murmured, taking in the brand-new king-size bed, the pickled pine desk and chair and the light green, gray and white miniblinds. She stared back at the living room, seeing a repeat of the same color scheme, with a few candy-apple red accents and crisp white plantation shutters on the windows.

"Pops said that he was pretty sure your father wanted to live here." Sara peeked into the bathroom. "Permanently."

"Pops said that?" Casey was surprised and a little hurt that Pops would talk about it with Sara and not her. Sara moved to the kitchen and looked inside the brand-new, and very empty, refrigerator.

"He also said that it didn't matter to him who you brought home, Pops was sure you wouldn't kick him out just because of a little bloodline." Sara looked over her shoulder, her expression showing her concern. "Would you?"

"Of course not!" Casey explained. "Pops raised me. He's my family as much as the boys are. I can't imagine life without him to harass me."

Sara smiled. "Good. That's exactly what I told him."

"And what did he say?"

"He said he thought so, too."

Casey followed the older woman around the kitchen, looking in the pantry, checking out the overhead cabinets, one of which was filled with a small set of green-and-white dishes, glasses, and pots and pans.

She and Sara looked at each other. "He did this as a gift to me, Sara," Casey said, as if it was the perfect explanation to her own unspoken questions. "He said that when he left, I'd be able to rent it out for the extra income."

Sara nodded, but her eyes didn't lie quite as well. They were definitely skeptical. "Right."

"You don't think so, do you?"

"No."

Casey frowned, looking around the once-no-better-than-a-storage area. It was an apartment any single person would envy. "But why wouldn't he stand by his word?"

"Pops told me that you hated your father's dismal apartment so much, you refused to stay there."

"It was awful," Casey confirmed. "It was filled with my mother's old furniture from twenty-five years ago!"

Sara opened her arms and encompassed the room. "Look around you. Everything is new and beautiful." She glanced inside the trash compactor. "*You* don't even have one of these," Sara muttered just below her breath. Then she continued with her tirade. "Now, if he hasn't spent a dime on his own apartment, and it's dismal—" her brow shot up for Casey's confirming nod "—then he's going to fall in love with *this* place."

"But he said he'd be gone in a couple of weeks."

"Did he say that or did you?" Sara tilted her head and her usually soft brown eyes were sharp as they forced her to remember the conversation.

"I did," she finally and reluctantly answered. "I assumed he would only take a few weeks to recuperate. In fact, I think I told him that I wouldn't have Pops disturbed, because Pops was a part of my family, which indicated that the Colonel was not."

"Sounds like a challenge to me." Sara rested against the windowsill. "And Pops said that the woman who picked out the furniture called today and asked if a once-a-week housekeeper could be found."

"For what?"

"To start with, to wash the new stuff and put linens on the bed and fresh towels in the bath. I told Pops to tell them yes, and I'd do it." Her smile crinkled the corners of her eyes mischievously. "For a right good price, naturally."

Casey looked shocked. "You're working as a *maid* for my father?"

Sara laughed. "You bet! It'll supplement my retirement check for a month or so. Besides, if I'm right about this, you may have a renter for a lot longer than you think."

"'Renter'?"

"Isn't that what your father said—something about he would fix and furnish this apartment, then give it to you as a gift so you could rent it out for extra income? Who would be the perfect renter, then?"

"The Colonel," Casey replied with a heavy sigh. "I get the picture."

"Bingo." Sara's smile drooped. "Sorry, darlin'. You know I'd do anything I could for you, including poison the old man, but I think your best bet is to confront him the first day he's here. Set up your rules and let him know you intend to make him stick to them. Otherwise, you'll have a boarder for life—one that doesn't cook or take care of the boys."

That thought was truly sobering.

"Or, you may lose the help you've already got," Sara added gently, reminding Casey of Pops's feelings.

"I'm in a mess, Sara. A true mess. If I allow my father to rent from me, I'll lose Pops, and I couldn't do that. He's always been there for me and I love him. But if I force my father to leave, I'll feel guilty for the rest of my life."

"Darlin', half the things we do, we usually feel guilty about," Sara said sympathetically. "But when you get older, your regrets are usually about the things you *didn't* do. So, set your boundaries with this old . . . man, and you won't have to worry about regrets later."

"I'll give it my best shot, Sara." Casey grinned, thankful that she had such a wise and caring friend. "Thanks. Again."

"You're welcome. Again." Sara's smile peeped through. "Now, while you're at it, grab those towels on the couch and I'll get the sheets. I've got to get these things into the washer, then set them up. You've got company coming."

"Right."

Casey did as she was told, then returned to her house. Rock and roll spewed out from the old stereo, and as she walked past the boys lounging on the floor doing their homework, she flipped the sound down.

"Ah, Mom," Jason said, but neither looked up.

"Ah, Jason," she mimicked, continuing through to the kitchen.

Pops was stirring something on the front burner of the stove.

"Soup?"

"Stew," he corrected, taking a deep sniff of the aroma. Casey was constantly amazed at how accurate his nose was in coming up with the perfect blend of spices in his culinary creations.

"What's the difference?"

"A lot when I make it," he teased. "So what's new, young lady?"

She sat herself on the ceramic-topped counter and watched Pops add another dab of something. It was as good a time as ever to talk about what was bothering them both. "Sara told me she's going to work for the Colonel while he's here."

Pops didn't turn around. "Humph."

"I told her he wouldn't be here long enough to nest."

He peered at her over his bifocals. "What makes you say that?"

She had to be honest. "Wishful thinking?"

Pops returned to his cooking pot. "Humph."

"Pops," she began, thinking that plunging right in was better than beating around the bush. "I love you."

He grabbed a wooden spoon and sipped at his concoction. "I know."

"More than anything except the boys."

"I know."

He wasn't going to give an inch. She waited a moment. "I just wanted you to know."

With careful precision, he set the spoon down on the counter and turned to her. His wrinkled face looked even more solemn than necessary and it hurt her to realize how much he'd aged in the past five years. Had taking care of two boys and a half-absent mom worn him out? She prayed not.

"Listen, daughter dear," he said, and she reveled in his old pet name for her. "I know this man is your father. I know he has a need to get in touch with you and your kin, because they're his by blood. I also know that blood doesn't mean a lot when it comes to matters of the heart."

Casey slid off the counter and walked into his always-open arms. "And you know that I love you," she finished.

"Right." His voice sounded muffled by her hair, but thick in tone. "And I know that whatever my fears are, they are not based on fact. It's just sheer terror for the ones I love."

"Unnecessary sheer terror," she corrected gently.

"Probably." He pulled away. "But that doesn't mean that you have to worry about me. We'll manage—all of us."

Loving warmth spread through her body, releasing the pressure of worry from her. Despite everything, Pops understood that she was in an awkward position and wanted to do the best for everyone. And he knew that she loved him.

Nothing else was as important as that.

The rest would fall into place.

LATER THE FOLLOWING afternoon, however, she looked out her bedroom window and saw a shiny red Corvette pull into her driveway. All thoughts of Pops and the boys fled. In their place was the fact that Matt had driven her father to her house from San Antonio.

Matt would be spending the night.

She set all apprehensions aside. He'd only be here a little while, so she might as well enjoy what the fates had handed her.

A smile lit her eyes and her heart as she raced downstairs to greet her guests.

7

THE COLONEL, LOOKING more robust than when Casey had seen him last week, stood by surveying the house, satisfaction written across his face. When he saw Casey bounding down the back steps, he grinned and held out an arm.

"Good morning, sunshine," he said as he hugged her.

This childhood nickname awakened even more awkward feelings than his hug did. She wasn't sure what to do or say. "Good morning to you, too," she finally managed. "How are you feeling?"

"Better than I've felt in the last ten years. I'm not sure if it's the pacemaker or the company I'm looking forward to keeping." The older man leaned against the car and stared at her backyard where lush greenery and flower beds burst with abundant color. Then he spotted the stream that circled the gazebo and ended in a waterfall in the corner of the yard. "This is nice." Immediately he drifted across the yard, stopping to see it from every angle as he made his way to the gazebo.

But Casey's attention was riveted on Matt, who was walking around the back of the car, his expression enigmatic. She gave a little smile, but he never changed his solemn mien.

"Are you okay after the circus the crew must have caused this past week?" He bent his head toward her in that endearing way he had, and she felt her pulse quicken in response. "Did they drive you crazy?"

"I wasn't here most of the time," she admitted, wishing she had the nerve to reach out and touch him. Just to feel that he was real instead of a figment of her imagination would be reassuring. "Pops and the boys were the ones who suffered."

The frown disappeared from his forehead. "I didn't know until yesterday just how fast and hard they were working until Mac called to let us know everything was on schedule."

"Mac?"

"He's the contractor. He used to be the Colonel's sergeant before he retired and opened a remodeling company. His wife was the decorator."

So that explained the speed. "I should have known," Casey declared, turning to glance at her father as he continued toward the gazebo. "The Colonel pulled more than a few strings."

"He could have," Matt corrected. "But he didn't. Instead, he hired a friend for work that would have to be done anyway. Mac was more than happy to help. He respects your father."

"It seems that everyone does," Casey stated dryly.

"Everyone except a select few," he amended. She didn't miss the twinkle in his eye, however.

Matt opened the Corvette's tiny trunk and pulled out two soft-sided pieces of luggage. Just as Casey was about to reach for one, a van pulled into the driveway and her boys tumbled out.

"Mom!" Jason cried. "Swim practice took forever today! Is he here yet?"

"Of course he is, dumb butt. And the Major's here, too!" Jeremy punched his brother's arm as he stared up at Matt.

"Manners?" Casey reminded sternly. She was proud when both boys straightened up and pretended to be adults—at least for all of two minutes.

Jeremy was the first to speak. "Good morning, Major Patterson."

"Good morning, boys," Matt said, equally solemn. "Your grandfather is in the gazebo. Why don't you introduce yourselves while your mother and I take his bags into the apartment?"

Both boys took off at a run. As Casey was about to follow, Matt stopped her by putting a hand on her shoulder. "Let them do the formalities in their own way."

He was right. The boys didn't need her to introduce them. They needed to take this first step alone. And so did her father. He was either going to be accepted or rejected on his own merit, and nothing

Casey could do—one way or the other—would be asked for or appreciated.

Without another word, she led the way up the stairs to the apartment. One glance told her that Sara had done her job well. Place mats with coordinated cloth napkins were in matching holders on the countertop. Towels were draped on bathroom rods, and the bed was made and ready.

"Mac did a good job," Matt said, inspecting the walls and floors instead of the decor.

"His wife did even better," Casey added, then sighed, remembering her conversation with Sara about the length of her father's stay. She walked over to the window and looked out, seeing her father sitting inside the gazebo and the two boys leaning against the posts as they sat on the steps. She didn't know what they were saying, but she knew they weren't joking around. Besides, she couldn't imagine her father cracking jokes. He was too cold and reserved for that.

Matt stood behind her, slipping his hands around her waist, his warm breath fluttering against her ear. "Give him a chance, Casey."

"You keep saying that, Matt. But you tell me, does this apartment look like a temporary home?"

His fingers brushed her ribs. "I'm not sure what you're getting at."

"I'm asking you, do you think he'll be here for his recuperation and then go back to San Antonio? Or do you think he's planning on living here?"

"I don't see what difference it makes to the here and now."

"If you know he's staying, Matt, then you both lied to me. If not, then I need to know."

He refused to rise to the bait. "You'll have to ask him, Casey. I can't be a go-between here. I'm having a hell of a time just trying to get *your* attention, let alone act as a mediator between you and your dad."

She relaxed. He didn't know her father's plans, and that was all that she needed to know right now. And she hoped that if the Colonel hadn't told Matt, he wasn't planning to live here permanently.

Leaning against Matt, she reveled in the fact that he was here—with her. The past week melted away, now that they were alone together. A need to hold him became so strong, Casey could barely control it. Turning in his arms, she kissed him with all the pent-up longing she felt but couldn't voice. Her hands tested the muscles of his shoulders and arms, her breasts flattened against his chest, tightening and filling with intense need.

Matt groaned and pulled her tightly against his own hard, taut body. The kiss was long, yet it wasn't long enough.

Eyes closed, Casey pulled back and took a deep breath. She unclenched her hands, letting them rest on his shoulders. Her heart pounded. Apparently, its normal beat was erratic around this man.

"The service never made me feel this way," Matt confessed, a note of laughter in his voice. "Not even after a ten-mile march."

Casey wished he hadn't mentioned his career. Her heartbeat slowed instantly. This relationship would last no longer than her father's visit. She didn't want more. He was military. What match could be worse for her than a good-looking military officer who apparently had no family, no roots? Her heart sank to her toes at her answer. *Nothing.*

Matt watched her reaction. "Don't shut me out, Casey."

Her eyes widened, their blue depths lighting in surprise. "I'm not. You're right here."

"*I'm* here. You retreated."

She felt his frustration and wished there was some way she could explain without hurting him. Without hurting *herself*. She couldn't think of a thing to say, so she deflected his attention. "I know nothing about you," she finally said. "Tell me."

It was his turn to be surprised. Then his gaze narrowed. "What's the purpose?"

"Because I want to understand you better. I don't know anything about you except that you consider the air force your home and my father is a close friend. What about your family? Any brothers and sisters? Are you the oldest? Where did you grow up?"

"Careful, Casey. You might become interested in this military guy," he said dryly. "And we both know that would be dangerous."

"Of course, it would. That's why I'll never be that entangled," she lied. "Tell me."

He struggled with his response. "I was born in Denver, Colorado. As far as I know, I'm an only child. My mother left when I was two, then my father, in his usual drunken stupor, finally dumped me on his sister's doorstep two years later. I waited around until I was sixteen, then I took off for points unknown. My dear, sweet aunt and her newest beau waved goodbye and good riddance. A year later I wound up in Omaha, joined the air force and found a home. A real home."

"The military isn't a home, it's a career," Casey said softly, her fingers smoothing his hair.

"The air force is my home no matter where they move me. It fed and clothed me, taught me manners and how to get along with others when I couldn't get along with myself. It even gave me an allowance, trained me for a career, taught me how to be organized, how to earn respect." His hand covered hers and squeezed. "My so-called family never did any of those things for me."

"But you're still alone. There's no one in your life," she said, but it was more a question. Her breath caught in her throat as she waited for his response.

"I'm not alone. Until you came into my life, Casey, I was very busy being an active bachelor. Your father isn't the only person I'm close to. I've made friends all over the world. But your dad came into my life at a time when I needed guidance. He supplied the discipline I needed to learn to be a good soldier, a good person. I owe him a lot—probably more than I'll ever be able to repay."

She ignored the part about Matt's active social life. "But that doesn't mean Dad or the military can take the place of a family."

"I disagree." Matt shrugged. "It was *my* family."

Steps sounded on the stairs. Matt cursed under his breath, then stole one more hard and short kiss. "Some other time."

Her laugh was light and airy. "Some other time," she echoed, thinking that there was never a sweeter promise. It meant that she and Matt would see each other alone again.

The boys clambered into the room, then stopped. Behind them, the Colonel chuckled. "Wipe your feet, boys. Your mother inherited that look from her mother. It's best not to cross her. She means business."

Casey laughed, too. Then went to Matt, who was exiting the bedroom where he'd deposited the Colonel's luggage. "All's well, Colonel," he said, as if he'd inspected the place.

"Thanks, Matt," her father said, but his eyes moved from Matt to Casey questioningly.

"Mom, Grandpa said that if you say it's okay, he's ordering our favorite pizza for us, tonight. Is it?" Jason interrupted, practically dancing with excitement.

The boys were so quick to accept their grandfather. Casey reflected proudly that they were willing and ready for the changes life had to offer because of the love and security she and Pops gave them. It was at times like this that Casey wished Jerry were here to see what they had created—two rambunctious boys who were the whole reason for her existence. They were growing up so fast. Soon they'd be adults, with families of their own. For the first time, the quick passage of time hit her. In six years or so, both boys would be in college, leading their own lives. And she and Pops would be all alone.

She gave Jeremy's shoulder a hug, blinking back a sudden sheen of tears. "I think you can have pizza, but you'd better not let your grandfather have any."

Jason's eyes widened. "How come? Pizza is good for you. It's got all the food groups in it at once. Cheese, mushrooms, sausage, olives, bread. Everything!"

"Everything that I love but can't eat right now," the Colonel said, regret lacing his voice.

"Or later," Casey stated with finality.

"Well," the older man hedged. "Maybe once in a blue moon."

"But not during the two weeks that you're here," Casey reminded.

"Hit him over the head with it, Casey," Matt said to her under his breath.

She glared at him. What did Matt know about families, anyway? Turning her attention to her father, she forced a weak smile. "Okay?" She knew she was pushing, but she wanted him to say he was staying for two weeks and only two weeks.

"Two weeks?" Her father looked thoughtful. "It's a deal." Then he turned to Matt. "Aren't you going to work with Casey for two weeks?"

"*For* Casey," she corrected. No one took notice.

"Yes," Matt said. "I start next week."

Her father looked thoughtful again, as if chewing over a problem. "So you leave here three weeks from now."

Matt nodded. "That's right. Three weeks."

Both men turned to Casey. "All right," she said, resignation edging her voice. "Three weeks."

"Three weeks," her father repeated.

"Meanwhile," Matt said, "I'm not in the mood for pizza. What about you, Casey?"

Much as she wanted to be alone with Matt, she was worried about ignoring Pops, so she compromised. "Why don't you come to the Barbecue Place with Pops and me?" she asked Matt.

"Think you can handle the boys, Colonel?" Matt asked her father.

The older man nodded. "If they don't behave, I'll ship them to the brig."

"Good enough for me."

Casey went to the kitchen, where she had noticed a pad and paper in the drawer. "I'll write down my pager number in case you need it."

That done, she flicked on the newly installed intercom and called the house. When Pops answered, she told him about their plans for the evening. Pops was quick to wiggle out of them. "Sara and I wanted to see a movie, and this sounds like the perfect night to go."

It also meant she had the evening alone with Matt.

DINNER WASN'T THE object of the evening. Being with Casey was. Matt stood in the upstairs bathroom and stared at himself in the mirror. Without his uniform, he looked much like any other semisophisticated, forty-year-old man. He wasn't stupid enough to deny his own good looks, but he didn't pay much attention to them, either. And he had a certain amount of charm—he knew, because females pursued him. In fact, ever since he'd been an adult, he'd just *expected* women to like him. And he'd never been disappointed.

Until three weekends ago, when he met Casey. She hadn't wanted anything to do with him. In fact, she'd taken one look at the uniform that usually had a charm of its own, and she'd turned to stone.

Now that she'd warmed toward him, she'd made it plain that it wouldn't last longer than the few weeks he'd be in town. Her attitude didn't do much for his ego, but it would certainly make things easier when the time came to walk away. So why did that bother him?

The boys' voices in the hallway reminded him that he needed to take Casey out of here. Then, with the slow and careful attention to detail that he was known for, he would woo her. He had to for his own sanity, so he wouldn't be the only one who had a hard time concentrating. Three weeks of knowing Casey had caused emotional havoc in his life.

He had to hold back the grin he felt when he walked into the kitchen and saw Casey, her expression worried. Pops was bent over, looking into the freezer, with only the lower part of his body showing.

"Are you sure, Pops?" she asked.

"I'm sure, I'm sure." His voice sounded muffled. "I'll stay out of his way and he'll stay out of mine. It won't kill either of us."

"I know, but . . ." Casey still sounded unsure.

"What's up?" Matt asked.

Pops came out of the freezer, a white, butcher-wrapped package in his hand. "Eureka. Homemade turkey sausage." He looked over at Matt. "Would you do me a favor and get her out of here for a while? She needs a little diversion."

Casey looked as if she was going to start World War III, but Matt intervened. "That's my cue," he said. "I'm starved and can't wait to sit down in front of a large steak."

"We're eating barbecue." She sounded distant, still preoccupied.

"Whatever it is, I want it now." Matt went over to her and took her arm, leading her toward the front door much the way she'd led him out the first time they met. "Say good-night to Pops."

"My purse," Casey objected, as they walked out the front door.

"You don't need it," he answered as he swung her into his arms. The boys and the Colonel were at the back of the property, and Pops was in the kitchen. He didn't want to waste another minute not kissing Casey.

"You're beautiful, and you're in my arms. What more could I ask for?"

She tilted her head to one side quizzically, but the fire that flared in her eyes warmed him deep inside. "Food?"

His mouth came down to cover hers. "To hell with food. You're all I need," he said, just before claiming the kiss he'd craved for the past week.

Her mouth was so soft and tender, so very warm and willing. His arms tightened. He brought the soft-

ness of her body closer to conform to his hard contours—and they fit perfectly.

When her arms circled his neck, he groaned. When
she moved against him, he forgot everything except
how good and right Casey felt.

8

CASEY SPENT THE REST of the week wishing she had never met Major Matthew Patterson. And when she wasn't wishing that, she was hoping her father recuperated quicker than the average patient. Her life had been turned upside down by those two men and she wasn't sure what to do about it.

Dinner with Matt had been wonderful and frustrating. After a long moonlight walk and stolen kisses, Matt had left. Casey had spent the first of many nights aching for his touch.

How would she deal with her desires when Matt returned to work with her?

Although Jeremy and Jason saw a warmer, more human side of her father, the Colonel avoided close contact with her stepfather as if Pops had the plague. When they were in the same room together, usually the kitchen, her father stood stiffly by the back door, looking ready to run.

What was even worse was that Pops seemed to enjoy his "contagious" status and would purposely walk closer to his victim, taunting him with his nearness. Then her father would turn up his nose as if breathing germs, and wait for Pops to pass before he'd relax just a little again.

Almost every morning, her father stuck his head in the back door to say hi to her and the boys, pointedly ignoring Pops. Casey felt her ire rise when Pops would smile back, put a cup of coffee into the microwave and ask the Colonel if he'd like a heated cup. The Colonel wouldn't say a word, just give the other man a dirty look and step out on the porch.

Casey tried to ignore the entire thing, working long hours. After eating a bite and talking to the boys, she would flop into bed, dead to the world, only to wake up in the middle of the night.

If she wasn't dreaming of making love to Matt, she was dreaming of telling off her father. Neither action was taking place in real life. Neither desire was even being satisfied a little—dammit!

It was Friday night and Matt was due to arrive in the morning. She heard the boys return and begin to tell their newfound grandfather about their escapades at the skating rink. Pops and Sara were playing bridge with neighbors. Casey turned on the stereo in the living room and opened the front window so the house could catch some of the cool evening breeze filtering through the tall pines.

God, she wished Matt was here with her tonight. Not that wishing did any good. She might as well enjoy the thought that he would be here tomorrow, instead of dreaming for things that could not be.

She sat on the dark porch and stared up at the sky as the stars slowly peeped out from behind the curtain of darkness. Peace slowly infiltrated her surroundings. The high-backed rocking chair gently swished against the planked floor as she rocked. Gradually her muscles relaxed, and she calmed down.

Since Jerry's death, she'd felt alone. But no man had drawn her, had made her heart ache, until Matt had entered her life. No matter how much she told herself this affair was no more than sexual infatuation, she knew better.

It wasn't sex. It was love.

She closed her eyes to block out the stars. Swallowing hard, she faced the facts.

All her adult life she had declared her hatred for the military life. The constant moves, the rootlessness, living in a society where everyone had to conform to someone else's system—those were all things she never wanted forced upon her children. Those were things that stifled creativity and provided crutches to others who could only follow orders, not create them. Everything about the service was an anathema to her. Everything. Including the people who chose it as a lifestyle.

And now, here she was, in love with a man in the military.

She was insane.

She was stupid.

She was also so terribly in love she thought she'd die from it.

Casey blew her nose. All she knew was that she wanted to be in his arms and rest her head on his shoulder. Just for a little while—maybe just long enough to pretend that they could remain together.

Then she would end their affair. She promised herself that. They would never suit each other. Matt was military and there was no way she would ever, *ever* allow her sons to be brought up in a world where allegiance to the country was more important than family.

Besides, Matt would tire of her. After all, he was handsome and single. There were lots of women who would want to be with him. He wasn't going to give all that up for one woman with a ready-made family.

She'd give him a month and he'd be ready to run back to his ordered, sterile way of life. For him, this time with her and her family was just a diversion.

But what a diversion!

Her pulse quickened at just the thought of being near him again—in his arms and next to the thick, sure beat of his heart. She wanted to make love to him, but she also wanted to experience once more that wonderful feeling of being in tune with that special someone else. To laugh and talk with him. To make love all through the night....

Her skin felt flushed, then chilly in the night air as her body responded to the erotic images in her mind.

Unable to sit still, she got up from the rocker and walked the length of the porch.

When headlights broke through the darkness as they aimed down her street, she halted at the steps and wrapped her arms around the stout wooden pillar. Inexplicably, she knew....

The headlights swerved into her driveway, illuminating her for one fleeting moment before being extinguished. Her eyes were blinded by the light, but instinct told her who the driver was.

Then Matt was there, standing at the base of the steps, his gaze seeking hers for confirmation that he was wanted. Needed. Her sensual awareness was so intense it felt like burlap scratching against her sensitive skin.

Her fingers clutched the post supporting her. He was so damned attractive, and so very *male*. Whatever that word meant, he was the epitome of it. Waves of masculinity seemed to wash off him and roll over her, steeping her in his scent, his very essence.

It was as if time stopped as they felt each other's being. They were ten feet apart but they could have been ten inches. It didn't matter. The effect was the same.

She knew he was moving before he did so. Each step was taken with deliberate, sure movements. Each step stole a little more of her breath, a little more of her ability to move.

She watched him as if he were the earth and moon, unable to take her gaze away from him for fear he'd disappear. Logic was gone. Thought was gone. She was woman. He was man.

When he stood on the step below her, his arms circled her waist and he rested his tawny head on her breast. An unbelievable tenderness unlike anything she'd ever known flowed through her, giving strength back to once-powerless limbs. She cradled his head against her, resting her own head on top of his.

Her eyes closed and she wondered if this would be the feeling she'd have when she arrived at the gates of heaven. Such a wonderful peace, contentment and strange exhilaration invaded her being that she felt as if time had stopped.

When he finally looked up, she sighed, reluctant to lose his nearness.

"I needed to see you tonight."

What simple words to express so much, she thought. "I wished for you."

He cupped her face and turned it toward him so that moonlight touched her skin with luminosity. "I heard it."

She smiled. "And drove here from San Antonio in an hour?"

"I was too nervous to stay at home tonight so I decided to drive to a hotel just off the highway about thirty minutes from here. I was going into the bar for a drink and heard you."

He might have been teasing her. But she chose to believe him. "I'm so glad," she whispered.

"Come back with me."

"Where?"

"The hotel. Now."

Her response was immediate. "I can't."

"Yes, you can. I called your father earlier. He has the boys." His voice lowered. "Please, Casey. Come with me."

There was no decision to make. Reluctantly, she let go of him and walked into the house. The intercom between her father's garage apartment and the house was in the kitchen. She punched the button.

Her father's voice sounded as if he'd been laughing. "The Colonel speaking."

"Pops is playing bridge and isn't home this evening. Do you think you and the boys will be all right if I go out for a while?"

"Of course," the older man answered readily. "We're watching an old Marx brothers movie."

Matt came behind her and nuzzled her neck. With a great deal of effort, she put on her best parent voice. "Boys, you behave. You have my beeper number in case of emergency. Otherwise, Pops is at Sara's if you need him. You know your curfew."

The boys shouted back their agreement, sounding as if they were more than happy with the arrangement.

Her finger came off the intercom and she turned in Matt's arms.

Their kiss was soft, tender, caring. It was as if both of them were afraid to ruin the spell.

"Let's go," Matt said raggedly, placing his hands on her waist and pushing her ahead of him, out the door and to the car.

The ride to the hotel was silent. Matt's hand rested on her thigh as if without the anchor of his hand she would fly out the window. The heat of his palm felt like a welcome brand.

They didn't stop at the registration desk, but took the elevator directly upstairs. Matt touched only her waist until they reached the door. Once they entered the room, propriety vanished.

The intensity that had flowed between them so sweetly before, was now thrumming through her veins like a driving necessity so strong it had to be fed immediately. She complied—by instinct and desire. But most of all, by need.

Tenderness was gone, replaced by demand. The kind of tense, ragged demand that washed away all thought in a torrent of overwhelming desire.

Clothing was pushed aside rather than discarded. Hands sought direct pleasure points rather than taking care to seek and soothe. Caresses weren't a part of this coupling. Casey claimed Matt and he claimed her. The only sound in the room were groans of greed and a need so powerful that it could not be called love-making.

When Matt entered her, she was pressed between him and the wall. Her movements were as aggressive as his, as she clenched his hips and felt the tension building in them both. Single-mindedly, she pushed him on, craving that goal of release. And, when it came, she whirled out of control. As if from a distance she realized that Matt was flying with her, and she held on for dear life, feeling secure he would take care of her.

Eyes closed in ecstasy, she felt Matt pick her up and lay her tenderly on the huge, king-size bed. He kissed her eyelids, her cheeks, then rested his forehead against hers. His skin was damp, and it was with surprise that she realized just how little of it was exposed. For the most part, they were both still dressed.

"Casey? Are you okay?" His voice was a warm, whiskey-laden whisper against her skin.

Eyes still closed, she smiled. "Never been better."

His low chuckle wafted against her neck. "Good to hear a military man can do something right in your book."

"No comment," she said, unwilling to be drawn into a debate when she was feeling so lethargic.

His mouth nuzzled against her collar. "You've got fifteen minutes to recuperate. Then I'll buy you a glass of wine."

"You've got fifteen minutes to call room service and order that wine, because I'm not leaving this room until it's time for me to head for home."

"For now. Just for a little while, pretend this is home." His voice mellowed, soothing her body like warm, scented water. "And we have no problems to deal with other than the small troubles of day-to-day living."

Silence settled comfortably between them. Matt rolled over and covered his eyes with his arm. Immediately, she missed the comfort of his weight. Warning herself not to get used to him or the pain of losing him would be worse, she rolled over and got out of bed. Five steps later and she was in the bathroom, staring at her reflection. She was grinning like a naughty Cheshire cat—a naughty, *satisfied* Cheshire cat.

She washed her hands and placed a wet cloth on the back of her neck. With a critical eye, she studied herself. High-cut white panties accentuated her slim hips and thighs, and her white cotton blouse fit snugly at her breasts. Her hair was mussed; her makeup—what little there was of it—was gone. She looked as if she'd been made mad, passionate love to.

Her grin turned positively smug—she had been.

Startling her, Matt strode into the bathroom. He was wearing his knit pullover—and nothing else. As he passed her, his hand reached out and patted her bottom with a familiar, possessive touch. Then he turned on the shower, slipped his shirt over his head, and stepped in. Water sluiced down his body in rivulets, sheening his skin like heated oil.

The hunger she'd thought sated returned. It came tearing through her like a high-speed train, slamming every part of her with such force that she could hardly breathe.

It didn't take any thought at all to shed her blouse and panties, then step in beside him. From the sexy grin on his face, she gathered that was what he'd hoped she would do. With a pristine bar of soap held in his callused hand he lathered her shoulders and arms, over her breasts and down to her waist. His touch was taunting, soothing, hungry. Every emotion that was unspoken between them was expressed in silent gestures.

His hand slipped between her thighs, then moved to her hips, teasing, taunting, playing with her. Eyes closed, she leaned against the tile wall and passively allowed him to do what he would.

A low groan echoed deep in his throat as he bent his head to taste her budding nipple. She moaned as his tongue laved it, sending fire all the way down to her abdomen, making her weak at the knees.

"Hold on, honey."

She heard him, but for the life of her, she couldn't answer. Instead, she nodded.

"You're so wonderfully soft," he murmured, his hand tracing a pattern across her belly to the apex of her thighs. He sought and found the nub of her femininity. Lightly, rhythmically, he shifted his hand back and forth until she couldn't help but move in response. Her mouth opened in a mute cry, and he covered it with his own, taking her breath away and then returning it to her after it was flavored by his.

She reached for him, trying to pull him closer, but he resisted. "Not yet, honey. I'm so ready for you, I'd explode."

His hand continued its massage, his mouth seeking lightly over her shoulder and neck. Casey arched her hips, her breath came in short gasps, her heartbeat raced against her breast.

Just as she thought she would die from the bliss, Matt entered her, his body shielding her from the running water. Slick with soap, his skin stroking hers luxuriously, Matt brought her over the edge. She clutched at his waist and hips to keep herself from drifting away completely.

It was a long time before they managed to move—their slick, wet bodies cocooned in warm, foggy steam. It was even longer before Casey managed to step from the shower and wrap a towel around herself.

Matt did the same, wrapping a towel around his waist. When he looked at her, his gaze was not only soft and tender but surprised and greedy. "Will I ever get enough of you?" he murmured as much to himself as to her.

Casey smiled, her finger etching a rib. "Sooner or later," she promised. "But not yet." She moved to leave the foggy bathroom, but his hand on her shoulder stopped her.

"Why not?"

This time her smile was contagious. "Because I'm not finished with you yet, big boy," she teased. As she placed a light kiss on his still-damp chin, a light series of beeps came from her purse. She recognized the call of her beeper.

She punched the small button on top and her household number popped up. "So much for Eden," she muttered, dialing the phone.

"Hi, Pops, what's up?" she asked, trying to keep her voice light and breezy, as if she hadn't made love twice in one night and was barely able to stand up and tell the tale.

She must have carried it off, because Pops didn't spare his words. "That father of yours kept the boys up an extra hour because they wouldn't clean up the kitchen and return his living room to the order he thought it should be in," Pops sputtered. "Those same boys, I might add, who have swimming practice at six-thirty in the morning!"

"Did they make a big mess?" Casey asked. Pops was never angry normally.

"Paper plates, napkins, pizza boxes. That sort of stuff. It wouldn't have taken him more than five minutes to clean it up himself."

She glanced down at her watch. It was barely after midnight. "Are the boys in bed now?"

"Yes, but only after I went up and got them. The Colonel is still angry that I took them out of there. I know you've got better things to do than play judge and jury, but this isn't going to work if he's going to be so rigid about everything."

"I know, Pops. And I'll speak to him about it in the morning," she soothed. "I promise."

Pops continued grousing for a few more minutes. Then, satisfied that Casey would take care of the situation, he hung up.

With a sigh, Casey sat on the edge of the bed and replaced the phone in its cradle. Matt sat beside her, his arm around her shoulder. "Want to tell me about it?" he asked.

She would have loved to share the burden, but she couldn't. This was something she would have to work out on her own. She always had; she guessed she always would. After all, they were her children—her family. She shook her head to emphasize her answer. "No. I don't even want to think about it, yet."

His hand found the base of her neck and began rubbing. She closed her eyes and allowed his fingers to ease the tension.

"Lie down on your stomach," he ordered in a low, soothing voice.

She did as she was told.

Beginning with her fingertips, Matt massaged every inch of her arms and shoulders. When he reached her back, he undid the towel and exposed the rest of her. Instead of feeling chilled, she was warmed and relaxed by his healing touch. The tension that had knotted her body was gone. In its place was a healthy, honest tiredness that lulled her to sleep.

He whispered in her ear. "Go to sleep. I'll wake you when it's time to go home."

Again, she did as she was told. There would be time enough for trouble in the morning.

9

IT WAS ALMOST FIVE in the morning when Casey and Matt returned home. With the exception of the pool of light on the front porch illuminating a stray cat who'd found a home for the night, the house was dark and everyone was asleep.

They shared a few last, lingering kisses in the shadowy hallway before Casey reluctantly went upstairs to catch a few hours' sleep. Matt retired to the folding cot in the dining room, which had been turned into a temporary bedroom for him. It wasn't the Waldorf Hotel and it wasn't Casey's arms. Though Matt wanted the latter and would have settled for the former, he fell asleep immediately.

After four hours' sleep in her own bed, Casey spent the rest of the morning in the kitchen with Pops. Jeremy and Jason had left early for swimming practice and the Colonel wasn't around yet. Although her thoughts kept straying to Matt and the night before, she needed to tackle her family's problems.

She layered more lasagna noodles into plastic freezer containers. "We've got to have some compromise here, Pops."

"Fine." He stirred the meat sauce in the large pot on the stove. "Let *him* compromise. Our life was fine without him. It's up to that old goat to fit into the family, not the other way around."

They'd been at it all morning while Casey prepared extra meals for the freezer. As usual, Pops helped so both of them wouldn't be so rushed during the week. With the family going in so many directions, this once-a-month ritual saved everyone time and energy when daily schedules were tight.

"That crafty old man doesn't want to be part of this family. He wants to run us like he runs his platoon," Pops muttered under his breath, as he added a little more coarse-ground pepper to the pot.

"He's air force. It's squadron," Casey corrected absently.

"Whatever," Pops mumbled.

Casey took the spoon and spread sauce over the noodles and cheese. "Let's not judge too quickly, Pops," she said, knowing in her heart of hearts that he was probably right, but unwilling to confront that issue yet.

"Fine, whatever you want, Casey," Pops replied, finally losing some of his steam. "Just remember, that man disrupts our life-style. We'll all be living here for a long time. He's only here for a little while."

Casey leaned over and kissed Pops's weathered cheek. She knew it wasn't just the boys that Pops was concerned about; it was his own position in the family that worried him. "I know. That's why we need to go a little easy until the Colonel's caught on to our way of doing things. *We're* the family, Pops. We always will be."

With a sharp nod, Pops acknowledged her words. As she finished filling the containers of lasagna, he quietly began the cleanup process. Soon, Pops was back in his own small office and Casey was halfway through kitchen duties.

The boys were due home from swim practice soon, and Matt would be up soon. Her father hadn't called on the "squawk box" and peace was temporarily in the air, when Sara knocked on the back door.

"Hi, honey, how are you doing?" her neighbor asked as Casey gave her a quick, greeting hug.

"Hanging in there."

"Pops been giving you a rough time?"

Casey nodded, then blew a stray lock of hair off her forehead. It bounced right back. "But not without reason. My father kept the kids up an extra hour last night cleaning up." Casey placed a few more dishes in the dishwasher. "That isn't really the end of the earth, except that, because they went to bed late, they didn't wake up in time for their ride to swim practice. Pops had to drive them."

Sara raised a brow. "And all this is your father's fault?"

"It wouldn't have happened if he'd sent them to bed on time."

A perplexed look crossed her friend's face. "Doesn't it sound like the boys might have had a hand in this? After all, that entire apartment doesn't take an hour to clean, let alone throw away a few plates and a pizza box."

Casey's eyes narrowed. "You knew about this?"

Sara nodded. "Pops was with me, remember?" She diverted her gaze to stare out the window. "Honey, your father is a man who finds it hard to mix with your friends here, but he's not the monster Pops thinks he is."

"Does it matter who's right and who's wrong?" Casey asked tiredly. "As long as there is conflict between the two of them, I'm in the middle."

"Stand aside. Let them battle it out," Sara suggested. "They'll either come to terms with their place in your family or learn to truly hate each other. But at least there will be an honest reason for their emotions."

"Oh, wonderful." Casey poured a cup of coffee and put it in front of Sara, then reached for a fresh-baked lemon-poppyseed muffin and put it next to the cup. "As if those two aren't enough trouble right now. Just what I need is for this feud to escalate into an all-out war."

"Good," Sara stated with a grin. "Because I've decided to have a barbecue a week from next Saturday and all our close friends are invited—including your father and Pops."

"Are you crazy? Putting my critical father together with all the people I love could be disastrous to my health."

"I don't think so." Sara sipped at the steaming brew. "It's time your father met the rest of your family. After all, he can't get to know you without knowing your way of life. This is just as good a time as any."

"He and Matt are heading back to San Antonio at the end of that weekend," Casey said, wondering how one phrase could contain such pleasure and pain all mixed up.

"Then it can be my going-away party for them." There was a distinct twinkle in her brown eyes. "Besides, in a way, your father is the host of this party. I'm paying for it with some of the money he paid me for taking care of the apartment."

Casey had to laugh. Only Sara would come up with such audacious irony. "Is there anything I can do to add to the chaos?"

Sara's grin widened mischievously. "Just bring that good-looking Major and the boys to my backyard for the party. I'll handle the rest."

"Will do." Casey's words were a promise. But in her mind was the certainty that this party wouldn't work to mend the breach between Pops and the Colonel. Right now, she couldn't think of anything—or anyone—that could perform that miracle.

Sara was an optimist. Casey was a realist.

MATT WOKE UP A LITTLE before noon, when the boys came home and began the task of mowing the lawn. Windows throughout the house were open and an early-summer breeze ruffled the lace curtains. Knowing Texas weather, he was sure that in a few more weeks the house would be closed up and air-conditioning would drone full-time. But for now, it was a luxury to lie here, listening to the soothing, everyday sounds of a close-knit, old-fashioned household.

For just a little while, it felt comfortable, like when he was a kid and the day was just too good to do anything other than lie in the tall grass, watch the clouds race across the pale blue sky and dream. That was one of his few good memories.

He'd had too few days like that as a child, and it was wonderful to experience the same feeling as an adult. Especially knowing that he was in Casey's house, and she wasn't too far away. Especially knowing that he'd been with Casey all last night and would have two full weeks with her.

Placing his hands behind his head, he grinned at the ceiling. Casey was becoming his world, and so was everything she loved. That included this house and the grounds she had so caringly planted and tended.

Aside from the smell of newly mown grass, there were other scents in the air, too. Warm yeast mixed with what seemed to be tangy spaghetti sauce teased his empty stomach. He looked at the small table next to his cot where his watch was propped. It was almost noon—he'd had not quite six hours' sleep.

Last night, after Casey had fallen asleep on his hotel bed, he'd been too keyed up to do anything but watch her, marveling that anyone with as much depth and sweet sensuality would want to be with him. And she hadn't chosen to be with him because of his money or his rank or even his looks. In fact, she was with him *in spite of* those things. It showed just how much she cared. That was a pretty heady feeling.

She knew where he came from and she didn't cringe or try to salve his ego with platitudes. In fact, she had a few ghosts of her own that she was trying to deal with. She wasn't a lightweight intellectually, either. The way she handled her family and her career showed a unique sense of balance and quick thinking.

One of the boys—Jason, he guessed—yelled to his older brother and Matt's grin widened. Those boys were so like their mother. She had raised them with a lot of common sense, humor and love. It showed in every look and interaction between them. Obviously, they had the usual problems most kids had— rooms that needed cleaning, chores that were postponed, homework that had to be done—but these were all workable things. Nothing unusual. Somehow, Pops and Casey had successfully found an old-fashioned way to raise new-fashioned kids.

"You're crazy if you think I'm tying those limbs alone, Jeremy!" Jason cried just outside the dining room window. "That's *your* job!"

"Not!" Jeremy yelled back. "If you don't do it, I'm telling Mom about your lies to Gramps last night about how long we could stay up!"

"Oh, yeah? Well you didn't say nothing, so it's your fault, too!"

"Then I'm gonna tell Pops about your lying and saying Gramps kept us up to clean his place."

"You'll get in trouble, too," the twelve-year-old insisted. "You went along with it. Mom says that's just as wrong!"

"*I* didn't say it. *You* did." Jeremy's voice crowed with the last word. "So you'd better do it."

Mumbling and grumbling under his breath, Jason must have followed his brother's orders because Matt heard shrubbery rustling.

Apparently, even good kids held each other up for ransom.

Matt wondered if Casey knew the boys had lied to both their grandfathers. He'd bet she didn't know. Twelve-year-old kids didn't realize what havoc they caused by such small lies, but it couldn't continue. It was obvious tension between father and daughter had grown so in the past week that Matt would have needed a machete to slice through it. Neither one deserved the added aggravation of two boys who played one against the other.

Yesterday, he'd spoken on the phone to the Colonel just before driving up and "kidnapping" Casey. It was the first time that Matt had ever heard a tone of defeat in the older man's voice.

"She won't talk to me, Matt. Hell, half the time she doesn't even see me. And when she does, she smiles and pretends she's listening to what I'm saying, but all her attention goes to the boys or that jackass, Pops."

Matt had tried to soothe the Colonel's feelings. "You can't expect her attitude to change overnight, Colonel. She has to get to know you first. Just give her a little time."

"If my heart surgery had any impact on me, it was to highlight the fact that I'm running out of time. I don't have that much longer on this earth."

"Don't hand me a hard-luck story," Matt had intervened. "You know the doctor said you could go for another twenty-five years or longer, as long as you adhered to his regime of moderate exercise and strict diet."

"I also know how many times doctors are wrong. I'm an old man, Matt. Now is the time in my life when I want to be surrounded by my children and grandchildren."

Matt had clenched his jaw so he wouldn't say the words uppermost on his mind: *If you felt that way, why didn't you reach out to your daughter earlier? I saw the hurt and rejection in her eyes when she spoke about you. I saw the anger. Face it, dammit, and take your share of the blame.*

Instead, Matt had remained silent.

But at least he now understood the relationship between the man he most admired and the woman he desired. Both felt slighted. Both were afraid of confrontation.

That was really kind of amusing when he realized that both father and daughter could deal with anyone else. But neither could pull down the walls between them.

Matt didn't want to make the same mistake the Colonel had made by rushing Casey. He'd take it slow and cautious. She already enjoyed being around him. They laughed together. They were great in bed. They were right for each other. *At least for the time being,* he reminded himself.

For now, it was simple.

With that thought, he jumped out of bed, slipped on shorts and a shirt, then took two steps at a time up to the bathroom. He didn't want to waste any time being anywhere but with Casey.

But when he walked into the kitchen a short time later, he wondered if he hadn't been a little optimistic.

Casey's elbows were immersed in hot water as she scrubbed a pot big enough to hold three or four good-size lobsters. Although there was a slight breeze coming through the open windows and screen door, small beads of perspiration dotted her brow. The white ceiling fan wasn't adding much coolness to the heated area, but a glance told him that a couple of burners and the oven going full blast were tough competition to any early-summer-day's heat.

"What's going on?"

Casey glanced over her shoulder but kept scrubbing. "It's the Lund household's once-a-month cooking contest."

"Who wins?"

"Everyone in the house who eats. Especially me." She rinsed off the pan. "Coffee's only an hour old."

Matt poured himself a cup and leaned on the counter to watch Casey's endeavors. Apparently this was some kind of self-imposed punishment or a female superhuman ritual—he wasn't sure which.

She picked up another pot and began tackling the interior with steel wool. He watched with interest as her tongue slipped between her teeth to rest on her upper lip in concentration. One of the pots on the stove hissed and steamed, but she paid no attention.

"Lemon-poppyseed muffins are on a plate somewhere on the table," she muttered, the sound of her voice echoing into the large pot she held.

He glanced over, couldn't spot them and decided he really didn't want to look for them among the splatters of spaghetti and brown gravy, pots, pans and dirty bowls.

He looked back at Casey. This wasn't working out quite the way he'd thought it would. Where was her delight in seeing him, her kisses of greeting and low voice of welcome? The attention he'd been so sure of getting?

The stove pot boiled over and Casey dropped her scrubbing to tend to it. Matt watched as she pulled another large pot off the stove, then set aside the lid and skimmed foam off the top.

"What is that?" he finally asked.

Casey glanced over her shoulder, apparently surprised that he was still there. "This is meat and onions I'm cooking to make a vegetable stew."

"Now?"

"Now."

"Why?"

"So I don't have to do it when I'm dog tired and the kids are hungry."

"I thought Pops cooked the meals."

"Pops has a lot to do, too, Matt," Casey explained, turning down the heat and putting the pot back on the burner. "There are plenty of nights we don't want to cook or turn on the heat to do more than warm things. This helps."

He glanced at his watch, wondering how he was going to get Casey away from the house for a while. "How much more do you have to do?"

She wiped her brow with her arm. "Plenty," she answered tiredly, her mind obviously not on the same track as his. "I was going to show you the tools and plans for next week." For just a second she closed her eyes and he pushed away from the counter to take her in his arms. Then she opened them again and her far-away look stopped him in his tracks. "Look, the plans for Monday's project are on the dining room table. Why don't you study them this afternoon? Then, when I'm through in here, I'll show you the tools and setup in the garage. We need to organize the equipment every evening so we can head out early."

He wanted to hold her. He wanted her attention. He wanted her to look at him to renew the waning strength he saw in her gaze. He wanted to be her knight in shining armor and take her away from all this. Just like a hero.

"Casey..." He finally had her attention, but the words wouldn't come out. "I'll take a look."

She seemed relieved that he was getting out of her kitchen and her hair. "Great. I think it's all self-explanatory, but if you've got any questions, please ask."

He couldn't quell his feelings of rejection. He'd been dismissed from her presence by made-up chores that would keep him out of trouble and out of her hair—just like the boys.

That hurt.

When had he lost control of their relationship?

Instinct took over and he reached out for her, taking her in his arms for a moment and holding her close to his heart. Her head rested on his shoulder and once more he felt in control and capable of ruling the world.

Her arms wrapped around his waist and gave him a light squeeze. But less than a minute later she stepped back and kissed his chin. "Thanks, Matt," she said huskily. "I needed that." She headed for the fridge. "Don't forget those plans," she called over her shoulder as she opened the vegetable bin and pulled out bunches of celery and carrots.

Matt stared down at the empty space where Casey *used* to stand, then back at the woman he loved. Her rump was up in the air, her head hidden behind the partially opened door.

Last night she hadn't been able to get enough of him.

Today, she couldn't get rid of him fast enough!

It took another minute for him to tamp down his anger. The military had taught him never to go into battle without complete control of his emotions. Instead, he'd keep busy and stay away from her until she came to him.

Sooner or later, she'd miss him.

Then he'd *think* about making an effort to find some private time for them—right after she apologized for brushing him off so lightly.

Feeling unappreciated and disgruntled, but unsure what else to do, he walked into the dining room and unrolled the plans for next week's job.

IN THE MIDDLE OF THE chaos in her kitchen and her hectic, mental list of things to do today, Casey found comfort in the neighborhood sounds. On one side of her yard, Terry and his wife, also named Terry, were mowing and weeding their back lawn.

Looking over her sink, she spotted Sara sitting on her redwood bench table, a wide-leaf rake in her hand as she talked to the Colonel, who had his foot propped on the seat next to her. In the past week he would usually take a walk around the neighborhood at this time of day, only he must have seen Sara and gotten sidetracked. If Casey weren't up to her elbows in partially cooked food, she would rescue her friend from her father.

Jeremy and Jason, occasionally shouting at each other, were weeding the front flower beds. About half an hour ago, Pops had gone to the grocery store to do the weekly shopping. He'd be gone half the afternoon. When he returned, they would put away the groceries, clean up the kitchen and call it a day.

Casey didn't want to think of the fact that she still had to take the boys to a roller-blade party tonight. The only good news was that she didn't have to pick them up—another parent would do that.

That meant that after seven this evening and before the ten o'clock news when she was sure to fall asleep from exhaustion, she'd be able to spend some quiet time with Matt.

That thought brought a wonderful, reminiscent smile to her lips. Last night he'd made exciting, passionate love to her, then massaged her tired body to sleep. What a marvelous way to end a romantic interlude.

This morning in the kitchen, when Matt gave her a warm, fuzzy hug and a light kiss, things had been even better. In doing that, he'd silently promised to stay out of her way so she could get her main chores done.

What a wonderful, thoughtful guy.

Once more, he was making her rethink her stand on so many issues, and the military was only one part. After all, he was a product of that environment and *still* had the sensitivity to recognize her preoccupation and realize that her heavy work schedule was top priority right now. And so, being the understanding and compassionate man he was, he'd allowed her breathing room.

She wanted to cry at the thoughtfulness of his actions. She just didn't have time right now.

10

ON MONDAY MORNING, Casey unlocked the truck's passenger-side door and pretended not to watch Matt as he stepped in. Once his door was closed, she slammed the car in gear and pulled out of the driveway, heading toward Interstate Highway 10.

Matt didn't say a word. Staring straight ahead, he seemed to be fascinated with the view of the Houston skyline.

What in heaven's name had gone wrong? On Saturday, he'd been so understanding in the kitchen. And that night, when Pops joined them on the porch, Matt had seemed so tolerant of the fact that they wouldn't have their time alone, after all. In fact, he had seemed to enjoy Pops's company, laughing heartily at his jokes, telling a few of his own, and waiting for the boys to come home with as much interest as Casey had.

Shortly after the boys had returned and joined them on the porch, he'd gone to bed—alone. He hadn't sent her a soft look or a suggestive smile. At the time she'd thought it was strange, but recognized that two adolescent boys and a stepfather could put a damper on

any romantic relationship—especially one like theirs.
After all, she was first a mother and daughter, and he
wasn't used to living in a family situation.

But this morning! This morning he was distantly
cool, receptive only to information about work, and
seemingly anxious to get going. There wasn't one
word of a personal nature or one intimate look that
said, *I remember us together and wasn't it wonderful!*

While she darted in and out of traffic, Matt unrolled the plans and had another look. "The first step
is to lift the top layer of grass, right?"

Casey nodded. "I called the utilities companies and
they came out early this morning to spray the grass to
show where all the cables are buried. After we check
those, we map out the area with stakes and string.
Then we take away the center grass and form the
streambed. It's like playing in a sandbox. You can
make whatever you want."

Silence again.

"Did you put on sun block?" she asked, casting a
sideways glance at his tanned, muscular thighs.

"Of course, boss. You ordered it, remember?"

She smiled. "Just checking."

She had, indeed. Last night they'd had a discussion
on the problems of working in sun and rain. She'd
stressed the need for sun block over and over again,
then left some in the bathroom for him. She even car-

ried a spare tube in the glove compartment and had told him so.

Silence again.

She wondered if the Colonel had said anything to him, but decided that couldn't be it. If dark, concerned looks were anything to go by, her father didn't approve of her and Matt becoming more than friends, but she doubted if he would say anything. He had to know that Casey wouldn't tolerate that type of interference in her life.

Casey drove down the highway and wondered once more what was going on inside Matt's head. She wished she had the nerve to ask. She was afraid he'd decided he'd made a big mistake in getting involved with her, and now, regret was keeping him silent.

Well, there was nothing she could do about it. Matt was working with her for the next two weeks, and after that, he could take her father and return to San Antonio. None of them would be the worse for wear—none except her.

She loved him. She would always love him.

Casey blinked rapidly to keep her tears in their proper place. She *would not* break down. *Especially* not in front of him! *Never* in front of him! She was so thankful she hadn't said anything about her loving him. If he knew...

She shuddered. Matt wouldn't ridicule her, she was sure, but if he physically rejected her, she would hurt even more than she did now.

ONCE AT THE WORK SITE—a gracious, old-fashioned home in the Rice University area—they set to work. When it came to the work load and how to handle it, Casey was amazed at how well they seemed to read each other's minds. As a team, they operated as if they'd done this a thousand times before. If Matt had a question, it was posed in the most simple manner and she responded just as straightforwardly and directly. She didn't have to give long-winded explanations. She allowed him to draw his own conclusions or ask another question if he needed more of an answer. That method worked as well as they did together.

After breaking for lunch, they washed their hands at the outdoor spigot before Casey brought out a couple of containers filled with tuna salad and crusty brown bread. Juicy slices of mango with lime wedges filled another plastic bowl.

Forgetting their earlier coldness, she announced with a grand flourish, "Lunch is served, your highness."

Apparently he'd forgotten, too. His grin was wider than hers. "It's about time the peons responded to my order for a feast."

Both laughed, then dug in. It wasn't until lunch was completely devoured that Casey realized Matt had emotionally withdrawn once again. With swift movements, she began stowing away the containers and wiping utensils clean. After returning everything to her truck, she picked up the shovel again.

Monday's routine set the pattern for the rest of the week. They worked hard all day, then returned home to clean up and eat dinner with the boys and Pops. Occasionally, her dad invited Matt to eat with him in the garage apartment, and a car or truck from some well-known Houston restaurant would pull up in the driveway, deposit wonderful-smelling containers, then speed off into the darkness.

Those nights were hard on the entire family. Jeremy and Jason, naturally curious, wanted to know what someone else was eating. Pops considered it a personal affront that the boys did not appreciate what was set before them. And Casey was jealous of her father's ability to get Matt to laugh and smile when he hardly gave her the time of day.

When she saw Sara take the path to her father's garage apartment, and later, heard laughter filter through the air, Casey felt jealous and even more left-out. She could hardly keep from slamming dishes and pitching forks.

Ever since her father and Matt had entered her life, tension seemed to be her middle name. It was building up inside her like an arsenal full of explosives. By Saturday afternoon, Casey was wound so tightly she was just waiting for someone to say something wrong so she could have a reason to shout.

Jason and Jeremy must have been aware of their mother's unusual temperament, because they did their chores quickly and stayed out of her way. Pops was quieter than usual, too, doing what chores had to be done, then retreating to the computer room and working on the mailing list.

Late Friday night, Matt had taken off for San Antonio with her father in tow. The Colonel's incision was to be checked, then they would return on Sunday afternoon.

From the living room window, Casey had watched them disappear down the street. From the moment they left, the house seemed to have lost its sparkle. The next two days, though they were filled with housework and chores from the past week, dragged unbearably.

It wasn't until Matt's shiny red Corvette pulled up in the drive that Casey admitted to herself just how entwined her heart and mind were with Matt's mere presence. When he'd left for the weekend, so had fun and sunshine. It was a frightening revelation, giving her a glimpse of the future to come. If nothing else, it underlined the fact that she should be enjoying every moment of his being here. He'd be gone for good soon enough.

On the other hand, because the tension was so thick between them, she should feel good when this "relationship" was over. At least she'd know that she wouldn't see him for a long time and that his presence wouldn't tease and tempt her nights, or make her feel sad at the daydreams that would never come true.

Shortly after she'd gone to bed Sunday night, she heard Matt's car. With quiet steps, she slipped down the stairs and unlocked the back door. It was several long moments before he appeared on the back porch. He'd first made sure that her father was safely up the stairs and inside the garage apartment.

When Matt entered the kitchen, Casey stood in the doorway to the hall. "Is he all right?" she asked softly.

Matt closed the door and slipped the bolt in place. "Everything checked out fine," he said, walking toward her, stopping only when he reached her. "I missed you," he stated simply.

"I missed you, too," she admitted, unable to pretend otherwise. She felt buoyed by his closeness. Maybe these feelings weren't so bad, after all. Maybe . . .

"I don't like it when we fight."

"We weren't fighting," she corrected. "That was the problem. We weren't saying anything."

"I went to bed one night and you were smiling. The next morning I woke up and you looked at me as if I was in the way and not worth the time of day. I was angry for you treating me like an unwanted child."

"I was busy. I thought you understood."

"I'm trying. But it isn't easy, Casey. This is a lifestyle I'm not familiar with. Give me time. I've got one more week here before I have to get back to my own life and yours settles into routine again. Can we make it as pleasant as possible—for both of us?"

"It wasn't my fault you had such a bad week," she protested.

"No. It was mine. And then your father put his two cents' worth in, telling me not to get involved with you, and I backed away."

"What did my dad say?" she asked, feeling her temper rise. Her father had no right to interfere....

"He said that since I already know how you felt about the military, I shouldn't set out to deliberately hurt you or your family."

Her anger dissipated. The boys *were* fascinated with Matt's career, and did enjoy his attention almost as much as Casey did. "And were you doing that?" she asked.

He shook his head. "No. But it was happening anyway."

"I'll tell you what," Casey suggested. "I'll worry about the boys and me this week. You worry about them next week, after you're gone."

"But I won't be here to help."

"I know." Casey cupped her hands around his strong jaw. As much as she hated to think of next week, he was right. "It will be better that way."

He bent his head and touched her lips with his. Her mouth opened willingly, her arms formed a circle around his neck. Heaven was being in Matt's arms, she thought dizzily.

Then he pulled away. "Get some sleep," he ordered gruffly before he gave her one more quick kiss. Even in the dim light she could tell he was drawn and exhausted. "We have work in the morning."

"We have to pick up koi tomorrow," she said. "Which means we'll be at the fish farm all morning."

His fingers tightened around her waist, threatening to drag her close. Then, as if realizing what he was doing, Matt released her and took a step back. "I need some sleep. Good night."

Casey went to her own bed feeling elated. Now that he was talking to her again, she felt as if a weight had been taken off her shoulders. Although not as bad as the lonely weekend without him, last week had been hell. Matt's silence had hurt as well as angered. But now things had changed. They'd both had time to rethink their relationship. Obviously, Matt was as willing as she was to be close again. Thank God.

Monday morning was as frantic as every other Monday morning. She and Matt were on the road to the koi breeders by nine. "What kind of koi are we looking for? Big? Bigger?" Matt asked. "I know they're colorful Oriental fish, but they all seem to be different. And their price seems to vary from ten dollars to a thousand dollars apiece."

"Although they look like multicolored goldfish, koi are actually the name of a colored carp originally bred in Japan. Their price depends on size and color, and this customer has decided to try the small ones first so he can make mistakes while he's learning to care for them."

Matt nodded his understanding.

It took the better part of the morning to choose the fish she thought would best accommodate her customer. They were placed in plastic bags, extra oxygen was piped into the bags, then they were sealed. When the fish were transferred to their new home, the closed bags of koi would sit in the water for an hour or two, until the temperature of the water inside the bags matched that of the pond water so the fish wouldn't be too shocked by their new environment.

That afternoon, Matt and Casey traveled to a new project a few miles away. Matt remained fascinated with the koi farm they had visited earlier, asking more questions than her boys did. "How can people pay two, three or four hundred dollars for a fish, when a cat could jump the fence and eat their investment?"

"Conditions in the pond make it so that fish can swim deep to evade predators."

"And if the cat wins, they return to buy more?"

"Of course." She laughed. "That's why Japan smiles with every koi pond built."

After a full day of work, they returned home to two loud and active boys who wanted to talk to Matt about flying. Casey knew her sons had a bad case of hero worship and wanted Matt's attention.

Matt indulged them and ate with her family. Casey tried not to show her happiness over such a mundane activity, but her smile wouldn't disappear. Out of a sense of duty, Casey called her father and asked him if he would care to join them, but he declined her invitation. Pops said nothing.

For the first time in the past two weeks, the boys didn't seem to care what their gramps was doing. Casey sensed it had everything to do with the Major sitting at their table.

Pops questioned him about flying, and she was surprised to hear how much Matt loved it. He didn't come out and say so, but every time he spoke of various planes and techniques, his eyes lit up.

That evening set the mood for the rest of the week. Her father ate in his apartment or at Sara's. Casey thought it kind of her neighbor to extend such hospitality, especially since Matt ate with the family. Jason idolized every word the man said, while Jeremy was a little more circumspect about his feelings for the Major.

Casey fell more in love with Matt with every hour that passed. She knew she would sink into a deep depression when he left, but she'd deal with that when the time came. Not before.

By Friday night, Casey and Matt were both ready to escape family and find time for just themselves. After emptying the truck, cleaning the equipment and showering, Casey sat waiting for Matt in the gazebo. But it was her father who joined her.

"Mind if I join you?"

"Not at all," she said, smiling. "I'm just waiting for Matt."

The Colonel stepped inside the gazebo and sat down on the bench, stretching his legs out in front of him. "Cassandra, don't you think you'd be better off if you didn't spend so much time with Matthew?"

"Interfering so soon, Dad?"

"Yes." His answer was as straightforward as the military had taught him to be. "I'm concerned about you and Matthew."

"Don't be. I can take care of myself."

"Really? Is that why you're out here waiting for him?"

"Look, Dad," Casey began.

But her father looked more stern than usual. He stood and stared down at her. "I don't want you to be hurt, Cassandra. I love that boy like a son, but I know his faults. Matthew is a handsome man who has women falling for him all the time. I don't want you to get hurt."

Tears pressed against her eyelids and she blinked quickly. "Please, I'm a big girl now, Dad. I can handle this on my own."

Her father looked down at the floor for a moment. "I hope so, Cassandra. I sincerely hope so. But don't expect me to remain silent on this. I'll have a talk with Matthew, too."

"Don't, Dad. It's none of your business."

Without another word, he turned and left her in the darkening confines of the gazebo. But his words lay heavily on her mind as she waited for Matt.

UNDER THE PRETEXT of taking her to the movies, Matt drove them once more to the hotel, where they rented several of the movies it provided and made love through all of them—one after another.

They ordered hot fudge sundaes, had a pillow fight, then made love again. Tomorrow their antics would be nothing but memories, but tonight this was her reality.

They returned in the wee hours of Saturday morning, and Matt reluctantly left her. He'd promised to spend the day with her father.

Sara's barbecue party was that evening, so Casey did something she hadn't done in years—she spent the afternoon pampering herself. After a leisurely bath, she gave herself a manicure and a pedicure, painting bright coral polish on her nails. Then she curled her hair for the first time in months, and took special care applying her makeup.

The emotional effects were astounding, even to her. She hadn't done this much for and to herself since she'd worked in an insurance office just after Jason was born! It felt good, and just a little bit naughty to indulge herself so completely. Logic told her she should have taken this time for herself long before now.

The visual results were just as astonishing. Knowing she was pretty, Casey had always taken her natural good looks for granted and seldom wore much makeup. But now, with a touch of peach blush, fawn eye shadow and chocolate brown lash lengthener, her whole look had changed. It was a change that was enough for now.

That decision was verified just a little while later, when the boys knocked on her door. She yelled for them to enter and they did, sprawling on her bed as she put the finishing touches on her hair. Curled away from her features, it fell in easy waves to her shoulders.

"Wow! Where are you goin', Mom?" Jason asked. Then he frowned. "You gotta date?"

"Course she doesn't have a date, dumb butt," Jeremy stated disgustedly. "She's goin' to Sara's barbecue. Right?" He looked at his mother for confirmation.

"Right."

Jason grinned. "You're gonna look so fine, the Major's gonna drop dead."

Casey laughed. Leave it to the boys to get straight to the heart of the matter. "Think so?"

Both boys nodded. "Know so."

Jason, always fearless about treading on private ground, got her attention quickly. "If the Major asked you, Mom, would you marry him?"

Her pulse leapt at the thought before her emotions plunged to the bottom. She gave a shaky laugh. "What in heaven's name makes you ask such a question?"

"'Cause I think he'd make a neat dad. He flies planes and goes all over the world, and he likes Pops and Gramps."

All important criteria. "He also *lives* all over the world," she answered. "And wherever he lives, his family would have to move with him."

"Really?" Jeremy looked horrified. "I just started high school and I like it. I'm not going nowhere!"

"Anywhere," she corrected automatically. The topic of marriage had obviously been discussed between her sons. "And I wouldn't worry about it. The Major isn't going to ask me to marry him. Besides, I couldn't if I wanted to, which I don't. I can't move, either, remember? I have a business to run."

Both boys looked slightly relieved. Jeremy rolled over and began doing sit-ups. "But would you marry him if he said he'd stay in one place?"

"That's not the way the military works, Jeremy. You know that. Besides, it's not in the plans, honey. He hasn't asked and I haven't thought about it," she lied, going to her closet to pull out her outfit.

"Yeah, but—" Jason began.

Casey held up her hand for silence, just as she'd seen Matt do that first day she met him. It worked. She was glad, because she didn't want to hear any more from her boys. No amount of logic would make her feel better about trying to raise boys without a vigorous father figure. But, some things weren't a choice that could be changed, but a fact of life. This was one. "You both better get cleaned up. We're due at Sara's in half an hour."

Without waiting for their complaints, Casey took her new pair of shorts and blouse and went into the bathroom, shutting the door firmly behind her. The boys continued to grouse, but she heard them walk out her door and down the hall to their rooms. Then, leaning against the wall, she closed her eyes and allowed her thoughts to wander to Matt.

It would be heaven to have Matt in her life on a permanent basis. She'd be crazy to deny it. And her love for him could overcome almost everything—everything but living under military rule again.

Her eyes popped open. What was she thinking about? Matt wasn't in love with her! Her father was right; Matt had his choice of anyone, and she wasn't a contender. She was sure that he'd realized just how unsuited they were for each other.

With a heavy sigh, Casey dressed, gave herself a once-over and left the house.

THE MUSIC IN SARA'S backyard was little different from that of most Texas barbecues. Sara didn't care for country and western, so she had her favorite "oldies" station on, playing songs from the thirties, forties and fifties. A backyard speaker nailed high in a tall pine relayed an old tune, while Sara bustled around the redwood tables, placing trays of condiments in the center of each one.

Casey saw the boys sitting on the back steps with three of the neighbors' girls—twins Kara and Mara, and their younger sister, Amanda. They were all approximately the same age as the boys, and all had grown up together. She kissed the girls' mother, Kay, hugged their father, Jeff, and continued into Sara's kitchen to see what she could do to help.

Since sliced onions were ready to be served, Casey grabbed them and headed back out. In the two minutes she'd been inside, her father had joined Sara at the huge, barrel-like barbecue pit. He was busy turning sausages and hamburgers while Sara spoke quietly to him. He nodded twice and then she smiled.

Spotting Casey on the steps, Sara veered toward her. "How are you doin', darlin'? Pops said you've spent the day resting. It's about time."

Casey laughed. "I know. I'm feeling guilty about it."

"Well, don't. You deserve it and more." Sara looked around. "Where's Matt?"

Casey remembered hearing Matt's and Sara's laughter from her father's apartment and a stab of jealousy hit the pit of her stomach. "I thought you'd know faster than I would."

Sara looked surprised. "Why? I don't work with him, you do."

Casey opened her mouth to comment, but Matt's arrival eliminated the need for words.

"Hi, Sara. How's my girl?" he asked, giving the older woman a kiss on her cheek.

"I was just asking about you," Sara said as she returned the gesture. "Where have you been all day?"

"The Colonel sent me shopping." He put an arm around her shoulders and smiled at Casey. His eyes took in her hairdo and makeup, and widened in appreciation. "I did a little of my own, since I was kept so busy during the week. I only have the weekend to get things done."

"Just like the rest of the working world," Casey stated dryly. But her pulse had quickened at the sight of him. The look in his gray eyes thrilled her. She could hardly contain the smile prompted by his reaction to her "new" look.

He winked. "But I have a beautiful boss who is a virtual slave driver. She makes me do physical labor until I drop from exhaustion."

"I find it hard to believe you could be so soft. Perhaps your boss doesn't expect any more from you than she demands from herself."

Sara watched the conversation between the two as if she were in the middle of a tennis match. "Even her sons say she's a slave driver. Chores have to be done just right or they get grounded."

Sara laughed. "Knowing teenagers, it might be the least punishment they could ask for."

"They haven't run away from home, yet," Casey argued.

"Their mother wouldn't let them." Matt's gaze held Casey's as if there was an electrical connection. "And they'd never be allowed to enter the military."

Casey straightened her back defiantly. "Never."

"*I'd* let them," Matt said in a softer tone.

"You're not their parent." Casey's voice was cold.

"No," he said slowly, dropping his arm from Sara's shoulder. "I'm not." Before Casey could ask why he was provoking her, he turned his back on her and went over to the Colonel's side.

"My goodness," Sara murmured. "Do you always declare out-and-out war with him?"

"He started it."

"But you took the bait."

"You're darn right," Casey said sternly. "He's the Colonel's adopted son. Does that tell you what he's like?"

Sara grinned. "You mean smart, strong, stubborn, opinionated and sexy as hell?"

Casey gritted her teeth at hearing the truth. "Yes." Her eyes widened as she realized exactly what Sara had said. "Not my father, Sara. Matt."

Sara patted Casey's arm, then started toward the house. "Either one," she said over her shoulder.

Puzzled, Casey watched her go, wondering what in heaven's name Sara could see that would be sexy in her father?

Pops arrived with their contribution to the party— a large container of pasta and vegetables, and a tossed salad with her favorite mustard dressing. "Has the old coot been doing all the cooking?" he asked grumpily, nodding toward the barbecue pit. "I'm surprised he knows the inside of a pit. It doesn't fly or have bombs in it."

"Hush, Pops. We're at a party."

"Another year and we would have had enough money to begin renovating the garage apartment ourselves," Pops muttered as he set the dishes on the serving table. "It was supposed to be *my* quarters."

Casey couldn't take any more. Instead, she went over to one of her neighbors and sat down on their blanket on the grass. Talking easily to friends about nothing in particular was refreshing. The past weeks had taken their toll on her nerves and she didn't need any more aggravation....

DARKNESS DESCENDED gently. The easy-listening music seemed to blend with the evening breeze, seeping into everyone and relaxing them when the meal was over. Casey leaned back and watched the stars appear.

Terry, folding cloth napkins and putting them into her own picnic basket, watched the kids cleaning up the grounds. "Matt really got them organized, didn't he?"

Casey refused to look. "That's always been their job, Terry. You know that."

"Yes, but usually I have to force the girls with threats of violence before they all get motivated." She laughed. "If I'd known that all I needed was a tall, gorgeous man to bark orders, I'd have hired one long ago."

"You must have hit on the only asset in hiring a military man," Casey muttered.

"I gathered. Your dad won't speak more than five words to us, no matter what we do. Every time we've approached him, he backs away as if we've got a contagious disease. I can't figure it out."

"Really?" Casey hadn't been around during the day to see how the Colonel and her friends interacted. It had never dawned on her that he was as distant with the neighbors as he was with her. After all, he seemed to get along so well with the boys, Matt and Sara.

"Yes, and when I was talking to José, he said the same thing. He'd stopped over and offered his help and telephone number, but your father didn't seem to be impressed with the neighborhood." Terry pushed her hair out of her face and tilted her head. "Is he anxious to get back to San Antonio?"

"You'd think so, wouldn't you?" Casey gritted through her teeth. Her gaze sought and found her neighbor, José García, and his family playing horseshoes with Jason and Jeremy. José occasionally helped her on more complicated jobs when she had to work weekends. Otherwise he worked for the City of Houston as an administrator. He and his sweet wife had helped her out more times than she could remember.

"Well, I'm sure this is a culture shock to him. After all, being an air force colonel and all is an entire world away from our little corner of the earth. We're still living like we're in the 1950s, while he's on the edge of the future."

"He's on the edge, all right. On the edge of my temper," Casey muttered. Ever since her father had arrived, she'd been put under more pressure than she could stand. Hearing her neighbor confirm her own feelings just added fuel to the fire that was rapidly building inside her. And knowing that her father was right about Matt didn't soothe her temper any, either.

But when she glanced around, her father—and Matt—were not to be seen. It wasn't until she looked up at the garage apartment that she realized that, like many of her neighbors, he'd already left the party. She could see his silhouette in the living-area window.

Anger took over. She glanced around, then found Sara holding one of their neighbors' babies. With a step that looked more like a military march, she went to Sara's side. "Did he say his thank-yous?"

Sara's eyes widened at her obvious anger. "Whose?"

"The Colonel's."

Sara relaxed. "Your father? Of course. He was tired out and went back to his apartment."

"I saw. I was just checking," Casey said, a little— very little—of the steam leaving her. "Tell me, Sara," she asked, "do you think Dad's a snob?"

Her friend's hearty laugh filled the air. "Of course, he is! One of the worst!"

"I thought so." Casey turned and marched to the garage-apartment stairs. It was time to set the record straight. Her father had to understand just how important it was that he try to fit in with her friends. She wouldn't settle for less.

11

She took the steps up to the apartment two at a time and knocked furiously.

The Colonel looked as surprised at her being there as she felt at finally confronting him. He stood in a navy blue bathrobe, hands in his pockets. His feet were in matching navy leather scuffs. "Cassandra, is something wrong?"

"I need to speak with you."

He opened the door and Casey stepped inside. Matt sat on the couch, his arm extended along the back. But at her entrance, he stood. "I'll wait outside," he said to no one in particular as he passed Casey and the Colonel.

"What's the matter?" the Colonel asked. His voice turned to steel. "Did Pops do something to disturb you?"

"No. You did."

"Me?" His eyes widened. "What did I do?"

"You've kept my children from their scheduled bedtimes, you've insulted Pops at every opportunity. And now, you've ruined Sara's barbecue by being cold and distant with my friends and neighbors." She walked to the window and pulled aside the curtain even as her father tried to speak. But he didn't stand a chance. She wasn't through yet. "Those people you so glibly hold yourself above are my family now. I love them as if they were the aunts, uncles, nieces and nephews that I'll never have. That makes them pretty special to me."

"And where does that put me?" her father asked quietly.

"You're a new relative. I don't know you anymore. I don't even know what you like and dislike."

"But you know what *they* like and dislike?"

She nodded to emphasize her point. "Yes. If Sara is sick I know she won't eat a hamburger casserole."

"She has good taste," he muttered.

"And if Terry has a headache, I know that she can't take aspirin. It has to be a substitute. And she can't eat oranges, but loves apples."

"And that's what makes them special?"

"That and more."

The Colonel took a step toward her. "And what will it take to make me special, too?"

Her throat closed around her words. She swallowed hard, then continued, determined to make him understand just how important it was to their tenuous relationship that he like her choice of family. "Time, Dad," she finally managed to say. "Lots of time. And a hell of a lot more understanding toward those I love."

The Colonel stared down at her, his gaze so narrowed she wasn't sure she could read his emotions at all. "Including Pops," he stated.

"*Especially* Pops."

"Cassandra," her father began.

"Casey," she corrected.

"Let's not quibble over a name," he ordered in much his old way. "Did it dawn on you that those people who are your friends might not be ready to like me, no matter what I do? That they may be feeling an unusually strong loyalty toward Pops, without even giving me a chance? That this attitude you think I have might not be all my fault?"

"No, it didn't. Those people are my friends. Besides, I know you well enough to know that you've always been distant. But in this case, it won't work, Dad. Love me, love my family and follow my rules." She didn't mean to make it sound like an ultimatum, but it did. She wouldn't back down. Not now.

"That's hard, Cassandra. That's cold and callous."

"So was the cold shoulder you gave my friends."

The Colonel went into the small kitchen and poured ice water into a crystal wineglass. "Will Pops get this same talk?" he asked, before sipping on his drink.

"Something similar," Casey admitted, knowing he was right. Pops had to learn a little temperance, too.

"That ought to be an interesting conversation," her father murmured. "Just remember, Cassandra. There are always two sides to every story. You've never given me a chance," he stated sadly. "I don't know that you ever will. But you *are* willing to play judge and jury and convict me on whatever you consider evidence."

Her father took a small pill off the counter and drank the rest of his water to wash it down. When he looked at her again, she could see frustration and impatience etched on his face. "You were always slow to start and quick to burn. Are you sure this isn't one of those times?"

"I'm sure," she said. But inside she shook with reaction. His accurate appraisal of her personality irritated her. She wanted to tell him how wrong he was about her, but she couldn't. "We'll talk another time— when I'm not upset and you're not tired."

"Running away, Cassandra? I thought you'd stick around long enough to tell me when I'm supposed to leave here and never darken your door again."

"Another time," she said, barely able to walk to the door without her knees shaking. "Please remember what I said."

"I'll never forget," he replied, his tone distant.

Casey closed the door behind her and went slowly down the steps. But when she reached the bottom, she couldn't force herself to walk inside the house and talk to the kids and Pops as if nothing had happened.

Instead, she went to the gazebo and stepped inside its blessed darkness. Once seated, her entire body began to shake. Seconds later, tears from old hurts, old rejections, new nerves and newer confusion poured down her cheeks.

With her legs pulled up, Casey rested her head against her knees. Tears continued to fall silently. She hadn't meant to tell her father off like that. She hadn't meant to make their confrontation so personal. She hadn't meant to get so *emotionally involved!*

More tears fell but she ignored them. After all, *she* was the wounded party, here. Her father had left her by choosing the military over her mother and herself. Then he'd chosen not to become friends with her until he needed help.

Some father.

Heavy steps hit the gazebo entrance and she looked up, swiping at her tears. The full moon outlined Matt's strong physique as he stood at the entry, taking in her ravaged face.

"Oh, honey." His voice broke with emotion. He picked her up, then sat down and cradled her in his lap. Her arms circled his neck, as she buried her face in the hard contours of his shoulder.

Tears still flowed, but at the same time Casey felt comforted. Matt's strong arms held her safe and secure, his warm breath teased her wet cheeks, and his own particular and heady scent surrounded her, making her feel cherished. Slowly, between sniffles, Casey's tears finally dried up.

"Was it that bad?" he finally asked.

Afraid to trust her voice, she nodded.

"Did he beat you?"

Casey shook her head.

"Did he hang you over hot coals?"

A smile tugged at her mouth. She shook her head again.

"Did he tell you what a dirty rotten scoundrel you were?"

She finally found her voice. "No."

"Then what happened?"

"I accused him of being a rotten grandfather and father. He said I was ignorant, or words to that effect." She hiccuped, then told him of their conversation.

Matt listened quietly until she had finished. "Did he tell you about Pops and the boys?"

Casey looked up. "What about them?"

"He didn't mention that the night I 'kidnapped' you, the boys lied to him about the time they usually go to bed?"

"Are you sure?"

Matt nodded. "Positive. The next morning, Jason and Jeremy were busy talking about it under my open window, only they didn't know I was there. I asked your dad, and he confirmed what I'd heard."

New anger surged through her. "I ought to ground those little buzzards for the next hundred years," she stated grimly. "They knew Pops and I were angry with my dad, and they never came clean."

"At least they're not dim-witted." At her surprised look, he explained. "Would you admit to a wrong-doing if you knew you were going to be in deep trouble?"

"Probably not. But they shouldn't have lied to begin with."

"None of us should. We should all be model citizens and keep the world clean for the next generation and help others and turn the other—"

"Okay, okay, I get your message," she said. "But they're still in trouble."

"And once they find out your father told on them, they'll hate him for it."

"I'll tell them you told me."

"Oh, great," Matt said. "Then they can hate me."

"You can take the heat. Besides, it might be best that way." She was thinking what it would be like when he was gone.

Matt sighed. "You're probably right."

It hurt to have it confirmed, but at least they both realized just how futile their relationship was.

Casey kissed his cheek, loving the feel of his warm, slightly rough skin. He tilted his head and kissed her on the mouth, instead. Her arms tightened, her fingers easily losing themselves in his hair.

"Wait a minute, you said Pops and the boys," she said slowly, her thoughts only now catching up with her emotions. "What's the story on Pops?" she asked when she'd finally recovered her equilibrium.

But Matt wasn't about to let her off the hook so easily. Instead, his fingers played with the buttons on her blouse, undoing them, one at a time, as he talked. "No one is blameless, honey. You know that. If your dad is a little standoffish, it could also be the fact that this isn't his neighborhood, it's Pops's domain. Everyone here knows you *and* your stepdad. Friendships like that are hard to enter into, especially when no one is paving the way for the Colonel by saying he's an okay guy."

When all her buttons were undone, Matt's hand slipped easily inside and curved around one lace-covered breast. Pretending to be casual about his touch, Casey nodded her understanding as she watched Matt's expression.

"Pops and your father have been fighting for your attention, honey. So far, it's been a fight to the finish. And you and the boys are the prize."

"I don't understand."

Through the flimsy nylon and lace, Matt found her nipple and gently rubbed. "Did you know that every time your dad enters your house, Pops turns on the microwave?"

Casey tried to concentrate on what he was saying and ignore his touch. "So?" she prodded breathlessly.

"A patient with a pacemaker can't be near a microwave. It disrupts the heart rhythm."

Leaning back, Casey stared at Matt's chiseled features in the moonlit gazebo. "Dear, sweet heaven," she murmured as the consequences of Pops's actions finally sank in. "So that's why Dad's always hugging the doorway."

"Heaven's what I've got in my arms," Matt whispered, his mouth caressing the swell of her breasts.

But Casey could only concentrate on one thing at a time. "I just played the indignant, righteous role to the hilt. I must have looked like a fool."

"I doubt it. You sounded more like a concerned mother and stepdaughter."

"A fool," Casey corrected, her face heating to a blush even in the heavy night air. "I read Dad the riot act as if I knew it all. I was so pompous!"

"Welcome to the real world, honey," Matt said, dropping kisses up to the hollow of her throat. "Everyone makes mistakes. Including you and me."

"Yes, but . . ."

"No buts," Matt stated firmly. "Tomorrow, apologize to your dad, yell at the boys and explain to Pops that everyone has to get along. Once everyone understands that *you* are setting the rules, they'll do fine. They just want to know you care about them. Like little kids, they're competing for your attention. They want to know where you stand and how much you care."

"Of course, I care!" Casey exclaimed, exasperated. She knew he was right. But spelling it out just made everything a little easier to see and understand. "I just want peace between them! This fighting is pulling me apart."

"Tell them so and they'll do the rest themselves, honey. I promise," Matt said, his voice barely a whisper as he continued to sprinkle small kisses on her cheeks and neck. "But since you can't do any of that until tomorrow, what else do you suggest doing to while away the evening?"

"I could knit an afghan," she suggested, arching her neck to give him easier access. "Or I could computer-design next week's work."

"That's true," Matt agreed huskily, trailing a row of kisses along her collarbone. "Any other alternatives?"

He reached around Casey's back and unsnapped her bra. Once released, his palm caressed her soft flesh as if stroking velvet. Casey could hardly hold back her moan.

"A few more," she whispered into the darkness, arching her back and inviting his intimate touch to continue. "We could play horseshoes in Sara's backyard."

His warm hands stroked her back and ribs and belly. Then Matt stopped her breathing completely with a kiss.

Love, like the stream that surrounded them, bubbled inside her for the man who held her as if she were pure gold. The tears she thought had dried up suddenly returned, but this time they were because of the separation she knew was coming. Matt would soon be gone and she would be alone. All she saw ahead was heartbreak.

But the alternative couldn't be borne either. Being the Colonel's daughter was as close to the military as she could tolerate.

Casey opened her mouth to tell him this wouldn't work, but his finger touched her lips. "No, not now, Casey," he said huskily. "Later, much later, I'll listen to your arguments. But right now, I want to make love to you."

The need she heard in his voice was enough to turn her muscles to water. Thoughts about their unsuitability fled. Matt was right. She was with him now, so she might as well make the most of it. There would be time enough for tears in the future.

Casey lost herself in Matt's touch. With caring gentleness, he laid her on the bench and made love to her as if he were memorizing her, memorizing the two of them together. Without realizing it, she did the same, remembering each curve, hollow and scent to recall next week . . . next month . . . next year. . . .

Soft sighs and muted sounds from both of them echoed through the gazebo. And after, Matt didn't let go. Instead, he cradled her in his arms and trailed soft, loving kisses along her neck and shoulder. Her arms kept him with her, her fingers stroking the corded muscles of his back. Even his weight felt good on her, she mused, wishing for the thousandth time that he would stay.

But she knew better than to hope for the best. Bests never lasted. Matt would go on his way and she would continue on hers.

"A penny for your thoughts," Matt murmured, sitting up and pulling her with him. After rearranging clothing, he pulled her back into his lap and arms.

"They aren't worth that much."

"Since it's my money I'm spending, I'll be the judge."

Casey cradled his strong jaw in her palms. Staring into his eyes, she saw the same contentment she felt, as well as the uncertainty of their tomorrows. "I'm going to miss you so much," she finally admitted in a whisper.

Light flared in his eyes for a moment, but then it died. "Is that all you can say?"

"What else is there?" she asked, confused. He already knew how she felt about the military. As long as he was in the air force, there was no other choice. Besides, her father was right. What handsome man like Matt would even consider taking on a crazy family like hers?

"What else is there? What about admitting you love me? What about eating your words about the military? What about taking an honest look at it instead of only the bad? What about *us?*"

Saying the words aloud would only emphasize the fact that they would soon be apart. She couldn't bear that pain. "You know the answers."

Matt's withdrawal left her feeling chilled to the bone. "I guess I do," he stated quietly. Placing her on the seat next to him, Matt stood. "There's no room in your life for me. You've got too many other relationships that take priority. And I refuse to be number six or seven all the time. I deserve better."

"What about me? Don't I deserve better, too?"

"You won't get any better until you think you're worth more than last place in your family, honey." His voice was so sad she wanted to reach out and hold him, tell him he was wrong. But once again, *she* was the wrong one. Both her father and Matt were right. She still had so much to learn.

"Does all learning have to hurt so much?"

"Not always, honey. Only the stubborn ones get burned." He sighed and looked up at the moon. Without looking back at her, he spoke over his shoulder. "Your father is staying a while longer, but I'll be leaving in the morning."

With fresh tears in her eyes, Casey watched Matt walk away.

At the gazebo doorway, he stopped. "I don't need to beat myself up over my past. I came to terms with it a long time ago. But you still blame everything wrong in your life on things or people. In this case, it's the military and your parents. I won't watch the fight."

Before she had time to form an answer, he was out of the gazebo and halfway across the moon-drenched lawn. Casey remained where Matt had found her. She had a lot of crow to swallow. In the short space of two hours, she'd alienated her father, made love to Matt and had been shown how wrong all her conclusions were.

Casey knew she had much work to do in the next week. A talk with Pops was first on the list, then with the boys. Then with her father—but that speech needed to be an apology.

After that, perhaps, just perhaps, she could get in touch with Matt, and let him know how things worked out. She could also apologize. And then, maybe—she would tell him that she loved him.

No! her mind screamed. That would be too painful. Too much for her to handle. But the thought of living without him was just as hard to handle.

There was no real solution that came to mind. Matt was a military man and she would not subject herself or her family to that way of life. She'd just have to live with his absence.

THE FOLLOWING MORNING, however, when Matt stood beside his car and told her goodbye, Casey thought her heart would break.

"Casey," he said softly.

She raised her hand and cupped his cheek. She needed to keep the memory of what it was like to touch him. "What?"

"Nothing. Just wanted to say your name." He smiled, but it never reached his eyes. "I won't be saying it for a while."

She wanted him to say he loved her again. She knew he did. She also knew that he'd never utter those words again until she admitted she loved him. Matt Patterson was one stubborn man.

The words spilled out. "I love you so much it hurts, Matt."

His face creased into a smile. "Finally."

She nodded, her own blue eyes reflecting sadness. "But there's nothing I can do about it. I wish there was, but I know better."

"I'm not fool enough to think your love is strong enough to allow us to be together. Without you approving of my career, I can't see us making it together."

"I know."

His fingers wrapped around her shoulders and pulled her toward him. "But just remember this," he ordered gruffly. "I'm praying my brand will be on you forever." Then he did what he'd said, branding her with a kiss that was as searing as it was sad. His mouth was hot and moist and hungry, devouring her without a thought as to who might be watching.

She didn't care, either. Her soul was already crying for him, recognizing that they would not be together for a long time, and when and if they were, it would only be temporary.

She had no choices left.

Matt pulled back and stared down at her. "Take care, honey. Remember me."

It was an order. Casey could only nod. With tear-filled eyes, she watched him climb into his car and rev the motor. He was gone from her life in less than a minute.

He'd never be gone from her heart.

THE TALK SHE HAD WITH the boys was short and direct. They admitted they'd lied, and that they'd wanted to tell the truth but it had seemed too late. After a short lecture and grounding them for a week, she moved on to the next problem.

Pops seemed to be preoccupied as he pulled out the frying pan and began the Sunday-breakfast ritual of pancakes, sausage and eggs. Casey sat at the kitchen table and watched him for a few minutes before breaking the silence.

"Pops, did you know that people with pacemakers can't be around microwaves?"

He stopped in midstride and stared over his bifocals at her. "Yes."

Her eyes widened. Somehow she was sure he hadn't known. "Did you turn on the microwave when my father came into the house?"

"Every time," Pops confirmed.

Casey's forehead wrinkled. "Why?"

"Because he'd leave quickly."

"I know it's been hard on you, Pops, but—"

"No buts," he said, hand in the air. "We just don't get along. He believes I stole your mother from him. I know better."

"My mother?" She stared at him. "All this has to do with my mother?"

Pops nodded. "Sorry, Casey, but you have little to do with what's going on right now. Your father believes that your mother had an affair with me, then decided to leave him. He blames me."

"Did you set him straight?" she asked, almost as indignant as Pops. Her mother would never have done that!

"Yes. I told him that we started our affair *after* your mother called Germany and told him she was going to file for divorce."

Shock froze Casey. "Affair?" she asked weakly. "Really? I mean, are you sure?"

A twinkle grew in Pops's eye. "I'm sure. I was there, remember?"

She didn't want to know. No, that wasn't quite true; part of her was curious beyond belief. To Casey, her mother had never been an individual, but a nurturer.

She was sure the boys thought of her the same way she'd always thought of her own mother: kind of . . . neutered. Here was another humble pie to eat.

"What did he say?" she asked.

"He said he was sure she'd met someone else and that he wanted her back. I told her she had to choose between the two of us. She did and we began an affair that led to our marriage." He turned and began making batter. "Are you shocked?" he asked without looking in her direction.

"No. Yes. Well, a little," she finally managed.

"I wonder why? I'm not shocked at your affair with the Major, and I was younger than him when I met your mother."

Another shock. Casey felt her face redden and was glad he wasn't looking at her right now. It had never dawned on her that Pops or anyone else knew Matt and she were doing more than going to the movies. How naive she'd been!

The rest of what he said finally soaked in, and she blushed once more. She didn't remember Pops as being that young. Assuming her parents had always known right from wrong and good from evil was a childish reaction. She should have known better. Everyone, herself included, had to struggle to make decisions that affected everyone, including themselves. And sometimes they made wrong decisions and got hurt. Like her decision to have an affair with

Matt when she knew she could never marry him. She was lucky she hadn't hurt anyone but herself.

Pops began using a whisk on the batter. "We're all human, Casey, and we all have our problems. It wasn't until I got older that I realized all life follows patterns. Mine wasn't too different from others'. I met your mother, fell in love and married her. We raised you together and I had a wonderful life with her. What more can any man ask for?"

What more, indeed? she wondered.

But Pops wasn't quite finished. "Don't judge too quickly or too harshly, honey. Too often in life we have to eat our own words, and as a steady diet, they can become pretty dry and tasteless."

Casey remembered telling herself that she'd never fall in love with a military man. What a fool she'd been for being so sure of herself.

12

CASEY HADN'T HEARD one word from Matt since he'd left two weeks ago. Whenever the phone rang or a car stopped in the driveway, her heartbeat accelerated. Then, when she realized it wasn't Matt, her pulse dropped to below normal. Although she knew her father had spoken to him on the phone several times, she was too proud to ask how Matt was doing.

Nothing out of the ordinary had happened during those two weeks, yet so much had gone on. She'd had a chance to get to know her father without Matt distracting her. When she'd first gone to San Antonio to meet her father, she'd thought her childhood memories of him were accurate. In short, she'd believed she knew her father. That couldn't have been further from the truth. She didn't know Colonel Porter at all—she'd only thought she had.

Two days after Matt had left, Casey had received a phone call from Mac, the man who had done the renovations.

"I just needed to make sure that the Colonel was happy with what Mabel and me had done to the apartment."

"It's a beautiful job," Casey had confirmed. "But you need to ask my father, since he's the one who lives there."

"He wouldn't tell me, don't ya know," Mac had stated. "But he deserves the best, the Colonel does. My Mabel just thinks the world o' him."

"Have you spoken to him lately?" Casey had asked, intrigued with Mac's relationship with her father.

"Oh, sure. We keep tabs on him 'bout once a month or so. He's family." The man had hesitated a moment before continuing. "Please take down my number and if you need something or the Colonel does, then just call."

She'd promised she would, then hung up the phone. *Family*. She'd been so immersed in her own life she hadn't bothered to notice that her father had his own loyal friends, too. Now that she thought of it, the mail he received from around the globe, the phone calls from what she'd thought were co-workers—even Matt as a substitute son—all confirmed that her father had done the same as she had: Her father had surrounded himself with people he thought of as family.

She'd been wrong. So very wrong. Her father wasn't a loner; he just had a different circle of family.

Another thought hit her. Because he wanted to get to know his real daughter and grandsons, he'd cut himself off from the friends he had in San Antonio. Yet, while he'd been here, she'd never given him the slightest amount of emotional support to help him through his recuperation or to help him become acclimatized to his new surroundings. She'd let him fend for himself and he'd done so—very well, in fact—even making friends with Sara.

Finally, however, in the two weeks since Matt had left, she'd had time to come to terms with her father. Learning how to be friends was turning out to be easy.

Casey pushed against the wooden board, moving the porch swing with a little more momentum. The kids, including her own boys, had gotten together an impromptu game of tag football in the street, and most of the neighborhood were on their porches observing the activity.

Her father sat in a lounge chair beside her, watching the boys and laughing occasionally at their antics.

"Dad, did you ever fish?" Casey asked lazily. She enjoyed learning about his childhood.

"Always. I fished along the banks of the Mississippi when I was a kid. Why, I thought a fishing pole was an extension of my hand until I was sixteen."

She smiled with him at the sense of humor she hadn't known he had.

"Do you think you'd ever want to take Jeremy fishing?"

He looked surprised. "Does Jeremy *want* to fish?"

Casey laughed, remembering the many times her son had begged to try it. "Yes. He's always wanted to, but neither Pops nor I do, so he's stuck."

"I'll be damned," her father muttered under his breath. "There's a little town called Concan that has a set of cabins on a river just out of Garner State Park. We'll start there."

"That would be great," Casey murmured.

Her father chuckled. "And I thought he only wanted to learn about making time with nubile young women with braces and long blond hair."

"That's his second love," Pops intervened in a gravelly voice. He was getting over a cold and this was his first evening back on the porch in five days.

Sara crossed the lawn to join them, her gypsy-long skirt swaying gently as she strolled. Casey watched both men as they waited for Sara. It was amazing what two weeks had wrought. It was a complete turnaround for everyone—all except Sara. She'd known all along that things would eventually work out with the Colonel.

"Hi, everyone," she called as she came up the steps and sat in the porch chair next to Casey's father. She held out her hand, palm up. "Stanley, you owe me for last week. I'll take it now if you don't mind."

"Woman, you are the most money-grubbing female I've ever had the pleasure of knowing," her father grumbled as he reached into his hip pocket for his wallet.

"I know," she said sweetly. "And I don't want one of your checks, sweetie. I want cash. I have a date with a manicurist tomorrow."

"I ought to set Jason up as an accountant for you. He's getting so good at math he'll be a CPA before you know it," her father stated as he handed over the money. He'd been tutoring Jason for the past two weeks, and the boy's least favorite subject was just beginning to make sense to him.

"I can count, Stanley," Sara said sweetly, tucking the money into her bra. "And money is the easiest to total."

Pops broke in. "Are we playing bridge tonight, Sara?"

"Not unless we can find a fourth. Tootsie is down with your cold."

"I can play." Her father's voice was firm. "In fact, I can beat the pants off most players."

Sara looked interested. "Really? What a delightful image."

Casey looked shocked, but her laughter bubbled over anyway. It had been a long time since any of them had heard that sound, and they showed their relief by joining her.

"What time?" her father asked.

"About another hour?" Sara asked Pops. He nodded. "Just about dark."

They squabbled back and forth about the various methods and conventions they all used, each describing their own variation of the best game ever. Casey listened with a smile. Knowing she wouldn't be missed, she went into the house to pour herself another glass of iced tea.

Instead, she sat at the table and placed her head on her hands and closed her eyes. As usual, the moment she was alone, an image of Matt popped into her mind. No one would know just how lonely she felt inside.

Lonely for Matt.

In the two weeks since Matt had driven away, her life had turned around. At last, Pops and her dad now tolerated each other. Sara was obviously sweet on her father, and Casey's business was going great guns, with enough contracts to last her well into the fall, and more inquiries coming in each day. In fact, last week she'd been featured on a morning TV talk show in Houston, and that had brought her even more business than she could cope with. If this kept up, she'd have to hire an entire crew by next month instead of making do with José, who, as of last Friday, now worked for her full-time.

Everything she'd ever dreamed of was falling into place, and she was still unhappy.

Would she ever have enough to satisfy her? Of course, she chided herself. All she needed was Matt in her life. But Matt hadn't called or written.

A vast hole formed in the pit of her stomach at the thought of him. There wasn't a night that went by that she didn't dream of him holding her, making love to her, softly laughing in her ear or telling her how madly passionate she made him feel and what he wanted to do to her. Though no one was in the room, she could feel herself blush at the memory of his words.

One of the boys ran into the downstairs half-bath. A minute later, he ran out again. Her father said something and laughter filled the air. Even her sons seemed to enjoy the new addition to their family. Gramps had become an integral part of their life.

Nothing had been mentioned—by either Casey or her father—about his returning to San Antonio. By unspoken consent, they had decided not to pursue the question. Casey didn't know when this question would be resolved, but if the past two weeks were any indication, things would work out fine without her help. The big problems were between Gramps and Pops and it seemed that they were coming to terms with their relationship within the family.

Just as Matt had predicted.

Go. Right now. Right this minute! her mind cried. *Find Matt and tell him how wrong you were about everything.* It was ridiculous to go on like this. She needed to make apologies, and Matt needed to hear them.

Her father came into the kitchen and reached for the giant tea pitcher. "Are you okay, Cassandra?"

"I'm fine." She stood. "Dad, do you think San Antonio is a good place to spend a weekend?"

He stopped in the middle of filling his iced-tea glass. A smile slowly grew. "I think it's the perfect place." He motioned to the large pegboard on the far kitchen wall. "Don't forget to take the key to my town house and check on it for me."

"Do you want me to look up any old friends for you?"

"I thought you'd never ask," her dad said. "I need you to check on Matt. He doesn't sound well."

"Is he ill?" Her heart constricted at the thought.

"Down with a cold," the Colonel confirmed. "He's been sick since he left here. But I think it's time you two got together again and talked over old times."

"I thought you were against us getting together," she said, surprised at his candor.

The older man looked a little sheepish. "I had this foolish notion that if I was against you seeing him that you might do it to spite me."

"Guess what? It worked." Her grin matched his. She stood on tiptoe and kissed his cheek. "Thanks, Dad."

The older man shrugged like a young boy caught behind the barn. "I didn't do anything. Not really."

"Really?" she teased. "And all this time I thought you brought Matt into my life so I could see how nice and sweet the military was."

He looked stern and dictatorial, but Casey now knew better. "The military is *never* nice and sweet. It's a man's organization, fulfilling a man's needs and wants, giving him the dedication and desire to succeed. In other words, it makes men out of boys."

"I'm sure the WACS and WAVES will love hearing that," she replied, knowing her father was needling her. She'd learned a lot about him in the last two weeks. One thing she'd learned was that his sense of humor was well and intact; it was just slightly different from hers. Occasionally he was so dry that Casey had to stop and think about his comments to know whether they were real or just teasing. But she was learning, and in the learning, she was realizing just how much she and her dad had in common.

"Are you going?" the Colonel asked.

"Yes. Are you surprised?"

"Yes." It was a blunt, direct answer.

"Why?"

"Because, honey, no matter what else is going on with you two, Matt Patterson is military. All the way. I can't see him changing something that is so much a part of his personality."

"I know," Casey admitted. "I kept telling myself that I hated his career choice, but it wasn't really true."

The older man smiled. "I knew you'd come around, sooner or later."

"But I don't think I can live in it, Dad." God only knew, she'd given it enough thought. Her new thought was that she would think about that after she saw Matt again.

"How do you know?"

"I just know. Go sit on our porch and tell me that you could take this life-style away from the boys. There are neighbors sitting on their porches, cheering the kids on. They scold them, hire them for odd jobs and praise them when they do something well. It's like having a hundred pairs of parental eyes watching them instead of just two. Here, they have a strong sense of family."

Her father looked her in the eye. "And what do you see that's so different in the military? When a small group of people band together for any reason, they make a community, Cassandra. You did it here. The housing on any base does it there. It's the same."

"But your neighborhood changes."

"Yes," he agreed. "And you meet new people, bond with them for a while, then move on again. But the neighborhood process is the same. No matter where you are, the rules remain constant and steady. There's something very reassuring about that, honey."

"Maybe," she conceded, needing more time to ponder what he'd just said. Right now it made too much sense and she wasn't quite ready to believe that just yet.

Her father curved an arm around her shoulder and gave a squeeze. "Sometimes, love overcomes everything, including the air force. Give it a chance, Cassandra. It could be what you've been wanting all your life."

Her gaze searched her father's. "Do you really think so?"

He nodded. "Matt's lonely. He's been looking for someone as perfect as you all his life. He just needs a kick in the butt to appreciate the fact that he found you."

"Thanks. I think."

"I'm not supposed to say this, Cassandra, but I will, anyway. Matt loves you very much."

She looked up, her eyes wide and hopeful. "Did he tell you that?"

"Not in so many words, but I know. I've known Matt since he was just a teenager."

"I hope you're right, Dad. In fact, I'm banking on it."

But as Casey parked her car in her dad's town-house garage, she wondered if she wasn't being just a little naive. Surely her father was wrong. A man like Matt couldn't really love her.

Casey straightened her spine. It was time to face the truth—no matter what it was. Both Matt and her dad were right. She had to face herself like an adult.

Five minutes later, she knocked on Matt's door.

When he opened it, Casey was stunned. Matt looked like hell. His skin was drawn and gray, his hair was sticking up here, lying flat there. A two- or three-day-old beard darkened his jaw. A faded pair of pajamas hung limply on his slightly stooped frame.

"My God," he whispered, his eyes widening as if he couldn't believe she was real.

"May I come in?" she asked. He pulled the door wide.

Casey looked around. "Are you alone?" she asked, as she closed the door behind her.

"No," he rasped. "I'm having a party."

"You're sick."

"For over a week." Matt walked into the living room and collapsed on the couch. "I wanted to call you, but I couldn't. I couldn't even think straight."

"You need to see a doctor."

"I already saw one. The worst is over now. He tells me that all I need is bed rest."

Casey felt his head—it was a good excuse to touch him. He had no fever. "Go back to bed. I'll clean up here."

"You need to leave. This is no place for you."

But Casey had come this far, she wasn't about to back down now. "Go back to bed," she repeated. "I'll come see you when I'm through."

"It'll be my luck that I'll dream of you," he grumbled, shuffling out of the kitchen toward the bedroom.

Her heart lightened just a little. "You dream of me?" she prodded, wanting to hear more.

Closing his eyes, he nodded. "I couldn't wait to tell you how well I'm doing without you."

Her heart plummeted again. "I see."

"But it would have been a lie," he continued. "I haven't been this miserable since the day before I signed up for the air force."

"Because of me?" Her voice was a mere whisper. Hope grew again. She was almost afraid of the answer she might hear.

Matt gave a heavy sigh, rested his head on the couch arm, and put his legs up. "Wake me in an hour or two and we'll talk then."

In seconds, he was gently snoring. Casey stared down at him, acknowledging that this was as close to heaven as she was going to get. She loved him so much, she was finally willing to tell him what was in her heart.

The Colonel's daughter was all grown up now and finally ready to marry the Major and become a military wife. And all this was on the condition that he loved and wanted her and hers in his life. Amazing.

Two hours later she'd washed the multitude of dirty dishes, changed the sheets on his bed and cleaned the bathroom. She'd never been so happy, so sad, so uptight and so eager to talk to anyone as she was waiting for Matt to wake up.

She was busy checking the empty pantry when Matt's voice echoed through the house, sounding more like that of a spoiled child than a sick man. "Casey, where are you? Come here."

His tone got to her more than his orders. After all, wasn't that why she'd hated the military for so long? It taught to intimidate by tone better than anyone else in the world. "I'm in the kitchen getting the material together to check your temperature, feed you weak chicken broth that leaves you hungry and then ask you where in the world you found the stupidity to bite the hand that *might* feed you."

"If you want to do all that, then you'd better get in here in a hurry."

Matt had left the couch and was stretched out on the bed in a pair of navy blue underwear that left nothing to the imagination. His hands were behind his head, his tanned body propped against a stark-white pillow. There was a slight dampness on his shoulders and legs that told her he'd just stepped from the shower. Casey narrowed her eyes and stared at him. Despite his illness, he looked sexy as hell. And he knew it.

No one was going to use their good looks to get away with anything while she was around.

Calmly, she strolled over to the bed and yanked the pillows out from under him. Matt's head cracked against the padded headboard.

"Wha—!"

"Don't play your cute games with me, Major," Casey stated between clenched teeth. "You've been gone for two weeks and haven't called once. So, I came all this way to propose and here you are, giving orders as if I were your lieutenant. Wrong!"

Casey placed her foot on the bed and leaned her arm on her knee. "We all have choices to make, Major," she said softly, with a hint of steel underneath. "Yours is to either say no to that proposal or to be sweet to me every day of your life so that I can keep a smile on my mouth." Casey took a deep breath. "My choice is to propose, and if the answer is no, then I need to get the hell out of here so I *never* have to see you again."

Matt sat up, his gaze holding her still. He placed the pillows back against the headboard and propped himself against them. Then he opened his arms to her. "Come here, honey. Let me hold you."

Suddenly the fun and kidding were gone. Matt wanted to comfort and hold her, and she was more than willing to have him do that. Casey climbed onto the bed, then rolled into his arms. She closed her eyes and felt the overwhelming comfort of him as he pulled her closer to the length of his body.

For Casey, there was no other place to be. This is why she'd driven four hours, cleaned house and taken a giant emotional leap. This was the reason for everything Casey had done in the past month. Matt holding her, his mouth teasing her skin, his hands clinging to her as if she were precious cargo; these were what she wanted—needed—more than breath itself.

"Talk to me, honey. Tell me what's on your mind," he urged in a whisper.

Casey closed her eyes and sighed. She might as well get this over with. "I waited for you to call and propose to me. I was sure you would. After all the anger was over and you realized just how good we were together and that what we have is rare and all, I expected you to come back and ask me to marry you. But you didn't."

He kissed her forehead, his warm breath ruffling her hair. "No, I didn't."

"Well, when you didn't do that, you never gave me the opportunity to say no to your proposal."

"I know, honey." His voice was a whisper. "*No* is such an ugly word. Especially when it's spoken by someone you love."

"You see, I honestly believe I'd be a lousy wife for you. I thought you needed someone more feminine and helpless, more adoring and cutesy. It takes a special kind of woman to live in the military and make it, and she has to be thrilled with your rank. I'm not like that. In fact, most of the time I intimidate men instead of making them feel like kings. And I'm not going to change. I'm not very good wife material."

Matt looked down at her. "Who are you trying to talk out of this, you or me?"

"Me. You. Both. I don't know."

"Okay, let me understand this," Matt said. "You were going to propose but you decided you weren't worthy?"

"Not quite," Casey corrected. "I was going to propose but I decided you really didn't need me in your life."

Apparently he wanted to ignore that part, because he honed in on something else. "You knew I was still in the air force, and you were still going to propose?"

The lump in Casey's throat was turning into a giant-size boulder she couldn't get a word around. She nodded.

"You knew you'd have to move the kids and find Pops a place to live and lose your business and *still* you were going to propose?"

She nodded again.

"Why?"

Casey swallowed hard. After all her protests and accusations against the military, she owed Matt this one. "Because I love you."

"No," Matt said, shaking his head. "That's not enough reason for you to propose. There has to be something else. What?"

"You and Dad said it often enough, I just didn't hear you until recently. The military is your home just like my neighborhood block is my home. The people there are your family. It took a while to recognize that I did exactly what you were doing—combining people into a family relationship. The only difference is that the military tells you where your family is moving."

"Eureka," Matt said gently. Then, holding her tightly, he kissed her with every ounce of tenderness he had. Casey felt like curling toward him, around him, seeping inside his skin where she'd be safe for the rest of her life. It was an illusion, but a wonderful one.

When he ended the kiss, she looked up. "Is that a yes?"

"Not quite," Matt answered thoughtfully. "It's an 'I'll have to think about it, after all, this is so sudden.'"

"Take your time," she said with irritation. "You've got an hour before I head back home."

"In that case, tell me when it's my time to add sanity to this conversation."

"Now would be a good time," Casey said.

"Good." Matt closed his eyes and she watched as he leaned back, putting his thoughts together.

Her impatience gathered momentum, but she bit her tongue. Was he being kind? Would he turn her down? It didn't bear thinking about. With everything in her, Casey prayed her father was right.

Matt opened his eyes. "I resigned from the air force the day after I returned home."

Her body went numb. Her ears rang in the silence that followed. "You did what?"

"You heard me."

"Effective when?"

"Next month."

"Why?"

"I'd been thinking about it for some time. Then I met you and fell in love. I love you too much to lose you."

Casey sat up slowly, crossed her legs Indian-fashion and stared at him, wonder etched in her every feature. "You would do that for me?"

Matt smiled. "For us."

Casey returned the smile. "I love you so much I ache with it, Matthew Patterson."

"It's about time you recognized the facts of life, Casey Lund," he growled, wrapping his arms around her and pulling her back down into his arms.

"Now that I've admitted that I'd move with the military, do you want to hold off on your resignation?" she asked, almost as afraid of his answer to this question as she was to her declaration of love.

"No. I figure you're going to need me, honey. Tonight, around ten o'clock or so, your dad is proposing to Sara."

"Sara?" she repeated stupidly, her mind not shifting gears quite as quickly as she'd like. "*My* Sara?"

"The very same."

"Dear, sweet heaven, what will happen next?" she whispered, more to herself than to Matt. The news took her breath away, but she should have seen it coming. If she hadn't been so wrapped up in her own affairs, she would have known.

"Well, I imagine your dad will move in with Sara, and Pops will get the garage apartment he's coveted ever since it was renovated."

"You're right." Why hadn't she noticed all this activity? Was she blind? *Of course, you were,* a little voice said. *Ever since Matt entered your life you've been blind to so much, while seeing things you've never seen before.*

"Now will you stay and take care of me until I'm well?" Matt's voice broke into her thoughts.

"No, but I'll stay until tomorrow," she compromised.

"In that case, the order of the day is to make love to me."

"I thought you were sick."

"I was. But suddenly I feel better."

She laughed and dropped a kiss on his jawline. "In that case, *retired* Major Patterson, we need to follow orders."

"See," he said against her mouth. "I knew you'd grow to see the error of your ways in the military. All you needed was a little discipline—"

His words were cut off by a kiss that promised a wonderful future of bickering, laughing and loving. What more could make Casey content?

She'd found that one good man.

**Earth, Wind, Fire, Water
The four elements—but nothing is
more elemental than passion.**

Join us for *Passion's Quest*, four sizzling, action-packed romances in the tradition of *Romancing the Stone* and *The African Queen*. Starting in January 1994, one book each month is a sexy, romantic adventure focusing on the quest for passion...set against the essential elements of earth, wind, fire and water.

On sale in February

To banish the February blahs, there's *Wild Like the Wind* by Janice Kaiser. When her vengeful ex-husband kidnapped her beloved daughter Zara, Julia Powell hired Cole Bonner to rescue her. She was depending on the notorious mercenary's strength and stealth to free her daughter. What she hadn't counted on was the devastating effect of this wild and passionate man on *her*.

The quest continues...

Coming in March—*Aftershock* by Lynn Michaels
And in April—*Undercurrent* by Lisa Harris.

*Passion's Quest—four fantastic adventures,
four fantastic love stories*

AVAILABLE NOW: *Body Heat* by Elise Title (#473)

**Fifty red-blooded, white-hot, true-blue hunks
from every State in the Union!**

Look for MEN MADE IN AMERICA! Written by some
of our most poplar authors, these stories feature fifty of
the strongest, sexiest men, each from a different state in
the union!

Two titles available every other month at your favorite
retail outlet.

In January, look for:

DREAM COME TRUE by Ann Major (Florida)
WAY OF THE WILLOW by Linda Shaw (Georgia)

In March, look for:

TANGLED LIES by Anne Stuart (Hawaii)
ROGUE'S VALLEY by Kathleen Creighton (Idaho)

You won't be able to resist MEN MADE IN AMERICA!

My Valentine
1994

Celebrate the most romantic day of the year with
MY VALENTINE 1994
a collection of original stories, written by
four of Harlequin's most popular authors...

MARGOT DALTON
MURIEL JENSEN
MARISA CARROLL
KAREN YOUNG

Available in February, wherever
Harlequin Books are sold.

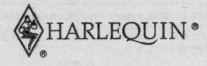

HARLEQUIN®

VAL94

NEW YORK TIMES **Bestselling Author**

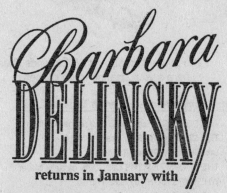

Barbara DELINSKY

returns in January with

THE REAL THING

Stranded on an island off the coast of Maine,
Deirdre Joyce and Neil Hersey got the
solitude they so desperately craved—
but they also got each other, something they
hadn't expected. Nor had they expected
to be consumed by a desire so powerful
that the idea of living alone again was
unimaginable. A marrige of "convenience"
made sense—or did it?   B0B7

HARLEQUIN®

Temptation

If you missed any Lovers & Legends titles, here's your chance to order them:

Harlequin Temptation®—Lovers & Legends

#425	THE PERFECT HUSBAND by Kristine Rolofson	$2.99	☐
#433	THE MISSING HEIR by Leandra Logan	$2.99	☐
#437	DR. HUNK by Glenda Sanders	$2.99	☐
#441	THE VIRGIN AND THE UNICORN by Kelly Street	$2.99	☐
#445	WHEN IT'S RIGHT by Gina Wilkins	$2.99	☐
#449	SECOND SIGHT by Lynn Michaels	$2.99	☐
#453	THE PRINCE AND THE SHOWGIRL by JoAnn Ross	$2.99	☐
#457	YOU GO TO MY HEAD by Bobby Hutchinson	$2.99	☐
#461	NIGHT WATCH by Carla Neggers	$2.99	☐
#465	NAUGHTY TALK by Tiffany White	$2.99	☐
#469	I'LL BE SEEING YOU by Kristine Rolofson	$2.99	☐

(limited quantities available on certain titles)

TOTAL AMOUNT	$
POSTAGE & HANDLING	$
($1.00 for one book, 50¢ for each additional)	
APPLICABLE TAXES*	$
<u>**TOTAL PAYABLE**</u>	$
(check or money order—please do not send cash)	

To order, complete this form and send it, along with a check or money order for the total above, payable to Harlequin Books, to: *In the U.S.*: 3010 Walden Avenue, P.O. Box 9047, Buffalo, NY 14269-9047; *In Canada*: P.O. Box 613, Fort Erie, Ontario, L2A 5X3.

Name: _____

Address: _____ City: _____

State/Prov.: _____ Zip/Postal Code: _____

*New York residents remit applicable sales taxes.
 Canadian residents remit applicable GST and provincial taxes.

LLF

Relive the romance...
Harlequin and Silhouette
are proud to present

A program of collections of three complete novels by the most requested
authors with the most requested themes. Be sure to look for one volume each
month with three complete novels by top name authors.

In January: **WESTERN LOVING**   Susan Fox
                                 JoAnn Ross
                                 Barbara Kaye

Loving a cowboy is easy—taming him isn't!

In February: **LOVER, COME BACK!**   Diana Palmer
                                     Lisa Jackson
                                     Patricia Gardner Evans

It was over so long ago—yet now they're calling, "Lover, Come Back!"

In March: **TEMPERATURE RISING**   JoAnn Ross
                                   Tess Gerritsen
                                   Jacqueline Diamond

Falling in love—just what the doctor ordered!

Available at your favorite retail outlet.

REQ-G3

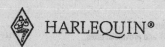

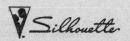

If you enjoyed this book by

RITA CLAY ESTRADA

Here's your chance to order more stories by one of Harlequin's favorite authors:

Harlequin Temptation®

#25449	THE LADY SAYS NO	$2.95	☐
#25461	TWICE LOVED	$2.99	☐
#25550	ONE MORE TIME	$2.99	☐

Harlequin® Promotional Titles

#83238	TO HAVE AND TO HOLD	$4.99	☐
	(short-story collection also featuring Debbie Macomber, Sandra James, Barbara Bretton)		

(limited quantities available on certain titles)

TOTAL AMOUNT	$
POSTAGE & HANDLING	$
($1.00 for one book, 50¢ for each additional)	
APPLICABLE TAXES*	$_____
TOTAL PAYABLE	$_____
(check or money order—please do not send cash)	

To order, complete this form and send it, along with a check or money order for the total above, payable to Harlequin Books, to: *In the U.S.*: 3010 Walden Avenue, P.O. Box 9047, Buffalo, NY 14269-9047; *In Canada*: P.O. Box 613, Fort Erie, Ontario, L2A 5X3.

Name: _____

Address: _____ City: _____

State/Prov.: _____ Zip/Postal Code: _____

*New York residents remit applicable sales taxes.
 Canadian residents remit applicable GST and provincial taxes.

HRCEBACK1

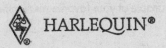

HARLEQUIN®